MODERN HUMANITII

NEW TF

VᴏᴌᴜᴍL ,

GENERAL EDITOR
ANDREW COUNTER

SPANISH EDITOR
JONATHAN THACKER

CᴏʀÍɴ Tᴇʟʟᴀᴅᴏ
Tʜᴜʀsᴅᴀʏs ᴡɪᴛʜ Lᴇɪʟᴀ

TRANSLATED BY
DUNCAN WHEELER

WITH A PROLOGUE BY
MARIO VARGAS LLOSA

AND AN INTRODUCTION BY
DIANA HOLMES ᴀɴᴅ DUNCAN WHEELER

Corín Tellado

Thursdays with Leila

Translated by
Duncan Wheeler

with a Prologue by
Mario Vargas Llosa

and an Introduction by
Diana Holmes and Duncan Wheeler

Modern Humanities Research Association
2016

Published by

The Modern Humanities Research Association,
Salisbury House
Station Road
Cambridge CB1 2LA
United Kingdom

First published 2016

ISBN 978-1-78188-244-3

www.translations.mhra.org.uk

CONTENTS

PROLOGUE BY MARIO VARGAS LLOSA

TRANSLATED BY

DUNCAN WHEELER

We have anthropologists to blame for the word uncultured disappearing from our vocabulary. In the past, a notion of culture was associated with advanced knowledge — in science and the humanities — a command of the arts, good taste and a refined sensibility. The anthropologist extended that meaning to all manifestations of a community's life — their beliefs, customs, rituals, vices and values — in such a way that we now encounter expressions in the press such as "the culture of feasting on human flesh", "smuggling culture", "football culture" and worse. Nobody is uncultured these days, we've all become cultured one way or another; this, no doubt, constitutes the apotheosis of our current civilisation, predicated as it is on frivolity.

In this context, Corín Tellado, the Asturian author who died just before her eighty-second birthday in 2009 was, in all likelihood, the most significant sociocultural phenomenon in the Spanish language since the Golden Age. What might ostensibly appear to be heresy — and from a qualitative perspective it is — ceases to be so if we begin to view things in quantitative terms. Borges, García Márquez, Ortega y Gasset, any of the most original thinkers and writers in my language that you might care to mention, none of them have reached as many readers or had so great an influence on the way in which people feel, speak, love, hate, understand life and human relations, than María del Socorro Tellado López, *Socorrín* to her friends. Aged nineteen, she wrote her first short novel, *A Daring Bet*, in Cadiz, an angelic tale in which a young navy cadet places a wager that he will succeed in kissing a girl, a gamble that pays off as a result of a power-cut in the middle of a party. By the time of her death, sixty-three years later, she had written another 4,500 novels — not to mention the countless radio-plays, soap-operas, photo-novels and films that were inspired by her works — that have turned the name Corín Tellado into a legend.

I first became aware of her in Paris in the 1960s, when I discovered that one of my nieces, who had come from Lima to take a course on "French Civilization" at the Sorbonne, had turned up armed with a small suitcase filled with novels, pre-empting the possibility her favourite author would be absent from the land of Balzac. This precaution was, in any case, pointless: as I soon discovered, a whole kiosk in the *rue de la Pompe* in the elegant sixteenth district was dedicated exclusively to the sale, loan and exchange of short novels by Corín Tellado; their client base were predominantly comprised of the Spanish and Latin American domestic workers of whom there were many in Paris at that time.

From that point onwards, I always harboured a desire to meet that extraordinary writer who, with her stories, managed to reach an audience to whom the "cultured" authors of Spain and Latin America would never have access. That ambition wouldn't be fulfilled until May 1981 when, after jumping through multiple hoops, I interviewed her for *The Tower of Babel*, a weekly programme I made for Peruvian television for six months. Securing the interview was far from straightforward. Her distrust of journalists was justified as she had already been ridiculed by various bully-boy hacks. When we met, at her home in Roces on the outskirts of Gijon, she wasn't at all as I had envisaged. An extremely dignified fifty-odd year old woman, she was short, modest, shy but forthright and completely unaware of the tremendous popularity she enjoyed in the media and popular imagination of over twenty Spanish-speaking countries or amongst the Hispanic communities of New York, Miami, Texas and California. This was a provincial woman, whose life had unfolded between Asturias, Cadiz and Galicia, dedicating her mornings, afternoons and evening to writing tales of falling in and out of love. A short-lived marriage had brought Begoña and Domingo into this world but, with the exception of this adventure and the break-up of her marriage, her entire existence was dedicated exclusively to fantasising and writing (or, more accurately, typing on her small portable typewriter) the romantic escapades sparked in her head. I talk of her short novels because, in line with her editors' demands, her books were never over a hundred pages long.

Her routine was strict and laborious. A housekeeper, a woman who had been with her since time immemorial and took care of all practical concerns, would wake her at five in the morning. She would straight away lock herself away in her study, a claustrophobic and windowless room with shelves crammed with her little novels, and would remain writing there for ten hours, with a brief break for breakfast at eight. She wrote without pausing for breath hardly ever making corrections. On emerging from her study mid-afternoon, she had fifty pages done and dusted, or, in other words, half a novel. She wrote two a week and, with that rhythm, her oeuvre already encompassed over 3000 books. Her problem as a writer, she explained to me, was that her head "worked a lot quicker than fingers could type". If her hands had been quicker, she would have written more, much more. Words were her living but, if truth be told, as is the case with all genuine writers, she didn't write to live but lived to write.

Beyond those ten hours of work a day, her life couldn't have been more monotonous and frugal. Four newspapers a day, a good siesta, a book from time to time, she'd visit a female friend on the odd afternoon, perhaps a film. On the rare occasion, a trip to Gijon to go shopping or to a restaurant, but always on the condition she was back home and in bed by ten at the latest. In the summer months, trips to the swimming pool and the occasional tennis match. There wasn't much more to tell.

When I asked about her favourite authors, she seemed uncomfortable and so I changed the subject. Her vocation wasn't to read, but to write. She didn't need to pause for breath, stories rolled out of the typewriter as fast as the words. That sudden paralyzing fear the blank page inspires in constipated writers was, for her, a complete unknown. Writing was as effortless and natural as breathing.

What was remarkable was that she didn't have the slightest hint of vanity. She explained she was always amazed when she thought about how many people read her, and it was clear that this was said with sincerity. Her editor had made out that her novels all had a print run of 30,000 and, although she knew the figure was probably much higher in reality, she wasn't bothered. If her editors pulled a fast one, she simply shrugged her shoulders. She told me that, sometimes, their demands were more irritating than those of the censors under Franco, who had taken a sledgehammer to her works on more than one occasion. This didn't bother her much: it was just a question of softening the incriminating phrases, and that was that! And, as evidence of her Franciscan patience and calm spirit in the face of a world that didn't always understand her, she told me of a blind protagonist she created for one of her novels. Her editor returned the manuscript with the order: "Operate on him". And she, of course, returned eyesight to the blind.

Although I never read the novels, I always respected her and treated her with warmth and gratitude. Because, thanks to her, hundreds of thousands, perhaps millions, of people who would never otherwise have opened a book, read, fantasised, were moved to tears and for a short time lived through that wonderful experience which is fiction. She could never have guessed it, but she was probably the last popular writer, in the fullest sense of the word, that which takes a variant (easy, basic, sentimental and sensational I know) of literature to the vast array of people who will never set foot in a bookshop, who flick through the cultural sections of magazines as if they were treading on hot irons, and view literature with a capital letter to be something long-winded that just sends you to sleep. With the death of Corín Tellado, we have likely seen the passing of a literature genuinely worthy of that epithet: popular.[1]

---

[1] This text is based on an obituary written for *El País*, and titled 'La partida de la escribidora'. Copyright Mario Vargas Llosa, 2009.

INTRODUCTION

BY

DIANA HOLMES and DUNCAN WHEELER

Romance is the most popular of popular genres. Until the globalised American brand of Harlequin swept across Europe then beyond (Australia, China, Japan) in the last quarter of the twentieth century, to become one of the most profitable publishing enterprises in the world, many nations had their own home grown romance industry centred on favourite authors: Barbara Cartland in Britain (1901–2000), Delly (1875/6–1947/9), the sister-and-brother writing team, in France — and in Spain, and later in Latin America, Corín Tellado (1927–2009). In 1962, UNESCO proclaimed Tellado the most read Spanish author alongside Miguel de Cervantes; official sales figures — discounting the proliferation of pirate editions that have sold millions in Latin America — are estimated at over four hundred million copies,[1] with The Guinness Book of Records acknowledging her in 1994 as the all-time best-selling writer in the Castilian language.

Even in her final years, attached to a kidney dialysis machine and confined to the house in Gijon, a provincial town in Asturias, Tellado dictated novels to her daughter, Begoña; at the height of her popularity between 1947 and 1970, she published at least a book a week to satisfy the unsatiated demand for novels which:

> [...] travelled in the pockets of both male and female workers who took the bus or the metro in the big cities, were to be seen in hospital waiting rooms, park benches, the exchange booths for comics and novels to be found not just in poor neighbourhoods but everywhere. Corín's novels competed with westerns in army barracks (in spite of the opposition from some officials that this was hardly virile reading for men). In some cases, Corín Tellado novels served as a pretext for striking up new social friendships. In the 1960s and 1970s, Spanish maids in Paris gathered together in specific cafes with the pretext of exchanging her novels and photo-novels.[2]

In spite or perhaps because of this popularity and cultural ubiquity, this grand dame of Iberian letters is the perfect example of Jo Labanyi's broader claim that:

---

[1] Alicia G. Andreu, *La construcción editorial de Corín Tellado* (Vigo: Editorial Academia del Hispanismo, 2010), p. 13.
[2] Ángeles Carmona González, *Corín Tellado: el erotismo rosa* (Madrid: Espasa Calpe, 2002), p. 109.

> [...] critical writing on modern Spanish culture, by largely limiting itself to
> the study of 'high culture' (even when the texts studied are non-canonical),
> has systematically made invisible — ghostly — whole areas of culture which
> are seen as non-legitimate objects of study because they are consumed by
> subaltern groups.[3]

Few twenty-first century bookshops in Spain stock any of her over 4,000 novels, with prospective readers having the choice of trolling the internet or thrift markets.

When intellectuals and literary scholars analyse her works, it is almost exclusively in sociological terms although none have carried out this endeavour with the rigour of, say, Richard Hoggart's *The Uses of Literacy*,[4] whilst neither they nor the authors of sociological studies in Spain traditionally deign to speak with the women who consumed these texts. A revealing exception is Alfonso Guerra, future Vice-President of Spain (1982–1991), who as a young man carried out a series of interviews about cultural habits with women who packaged olives in Seville in the early 1960s, the modern-day equivalent of the cigarette girls from *Carmen*; this was a harbinger of how and why his engagement with popular culture and a broad-cross section of society would be instrumental to his subsequent success in parliamentary politics.[5] Beyond the Iberian Peninsula, Cuban émigré Guillermo Cabrera Infante was puzzled by his daughter Anita's questions, prompted by her reading of Tellado's novels, about the identity of Jean de la Bruyère or what a marriage not being consummated entailed. He not only read and analysed some of her favourite books, but also published an interview with the twelve year old in which she concedes that the romances are formulaic but reasons that this does not prevent him from reading detective novels by Nero Wolfe or Dashiell Hammett.[6]

Paternalistic condescension is, however, the overriding tone of the two major Spanish academic books dedicated to Tellado during her imperial phase, both of them rife with impressionistic generalisations based on a limited corpus. Noting that hers are the only novels to regularly sell over 100,000 copies a week in Spain, Andrés Amorós observes the tendency for intellectuals to snobbishly disregard the kind of texts 'read by young postwomen on the metro ... and, in boring lectures, by female students and, in the privacy of their own homes, by virtually

---

[3] Jo Labanyi 'Introduction: Engaging with Ghosts, or Theorizing Culture in Modern Spain', in *Constructing Identity in Contemporary Spain: Theoretical Debates and Cultural Practices*, ed. by Jo Labanyi (Oxford: Oxford University Press, 2002), pp. 1–14 (p. 2).

[4] Richard Hoggart, *The Uses of Literacy: Aspects of Working Class Life* (London: Penguin Classics, 2009).

[5] Duncan Wheeler, 'Letter from Madrid: a Conversation with Alfonso Guerra', *The Political Quarterly* 87.3 (2016), 312–17.

[6] Guillermo Cabrera Infante, 'Una inocente pornógrafo (manes i desmanes de Corín Tellado), in *O*', by Guillermo Cabrera Infante (Barcelona: Seix Barral, 1975), pp. 39–60 (p. 59).

all women'.[7] Through his own admission, this Professor from Madrid's Complutense University bases his analysis on just ten novels, but he does at least attempt to engage with her literary output, criticising his colleagues for failing to do so; an infantilising tone nevertheless prevails as Tellado is posited as the antithesis of Bertolt Brecht, thereby providing the context for Amorós's argument that '[t]hese novels reflect, perhaps, modes of thinking and acting typical of those sections of Spanish society that are "stuck in the past", and don't show any signs of leaving it in the immediate future. Our criticisms are directed more at them than the novels themselves'.[8] The same paternalistic attitude is clearly manifest in José María Díez Borque's diagnosis of:

> [...] the need for escapism amongst the humble sections of society, because their level of happiness — measured objectively — is lower. The masses are docile, their capacity for judgement can be determined from above, but the challenge resides in determining the limits of that vague noun, "masses".[9]

This forms part of a broader heuristic trend aptly summarised by Janice Radway as 'the commonplace view that mass cultural forms like the romance perform their social function by imposing alien ideology upon unsuspecting if not somnolent readers'.[10]

Tellado conquered the Latin American market in the early-1950s through the inclusion of her fictions in Cuban magazine *Vanidades/Vanities*;[11] following the Cuban Revolution in 1958, the Castro regime sought the closure of women's and gossip magazines. The original *Vanidades* moved its centre of operations to Miami,[12] whilst the magazine was nationalised in Cuba under the auspices of the Federation of Cuban Women. Tellado continued publishing with the Cuban edition until November 1960 when she terminated the contract reportedly due to her disapproval of the nascent regime,[13] at which point the editorial team outed Tellado as an imposter, claiming the novels were written by a team of hacks.[14]

---

[7] Andrés Amorós, *Sociología de una novela rosa* (Madrid: Taurus, 1968), p. 11.

[8] Ibid., pp. 73–74.

[9] José María Díez Borque, *Literatura y cultura de masas: estudio de la novela subliteraria* (Madrid: Al-Borak, 1972), p. 18.

[10] Janice Radway, *Reading the Romance: Women, Patriarchy, and Popular Literature* (Chapel Hill: University of North Carolina Press, 1984), p. 8.

[11] Hubert Pöppel, 'Las reinas de la novela rosa en España y Alemania: Corín Tellado y Hedwing Courths-Mahler', *Lingüística y Literatura*, 66 (2014), 153–70 (p. 156).

[12] Alicia G. Andreu, 'Difusión y distribución de Corín Tellado en Hispanoamérica', *Hispania* 92.3 (2009), 624–34 (p. 625).

[13] Marisela Fleites-Lear, '¿Victoria contra Corín Tellado?: la novela rosa revolucionaria cubana y la ficción en *Mujeres*', *Romance Notes*, 49.1 (2009), 91–100 (p. 92).

[14] This dispute needs to be framed in a broader socio-political context. Although the Franco regime had initially recognised and applauded the Cuban Revolution, tensions came to the fore over the course of 1960 when the Spanish Ambassador in Havana established contact with

Vanidades was re-branded as *Mujeres/Women* in 1961, and continued to publish romantic novels ("novelas rosas") albeit featuring revolutionary protagonists; the magazine, nevertheless, denounced Tellado periodically over the following decades as the embodiment of false consciousness and bourgeois deviationism, responding in 1987 to a letter from a seventeen-year-old reader who says she wants to read these novels with a swift admonishment and an alternative (male) reading list featuring Balzac, Tolstoy, Shakespeare, García Márquez and the Cuban Manuel Cofiño.[15]

Synergies can, in fact, be found between the Federation of Cuban Women, the writings of Díez Borque or Amorós, and Germaine Greer who argued in her epochal text *The Female Eunuch* that: 'If female liberation is to happen, if the reservoir of real female love is to be tapped, this sterile self-deception must be counteracted. The only literary form which could outsell romantic trash on the female market is hard-core pornography'.[16] Revealingly, male critics in post-Franco Spain were generally less predisposed to denounce the seemingly overnight explosion of hard-core pornography than they were 'romantic trash'. The hegemony of the Communist Party and a Marxist inflected intelligentsia in the anti-Franco struggle as in contemporary criticism produced a situation in which popular culture was deemed to be feminised and, by implication, corrupted and corrupting;[17] this critical habitus paradoxically shared some of second wave feminism's critiques of the romance novel, whilst simultaneously almost completely ignoring the women's rights agenda, rendered as subservient to class struggle.

In contrast to the Anglophone world where the readers of romance novels are almost invariably female — Mills and Boon had a mailing list of 9000 names in 1967, of which only two were male —[18] Tellado did, as we have seen, have some male readers in Spain although this was at least in part the result of a limited range of accessible books in both economic and linguistic terms; her core demographic was nevertheless overwhelmingly female. If we entertain seriously the claim that romance 'provides a narrative form in which to address the difficult

---

anti-regime members of the Catholic Church. See Joaquín Roy, *La siempre fiel: un siglo de relaciones hispanocubanos (1898–1998)* (Madrid: Instituto Universitario de Desarrollo y Cooperación y los libros de la Catarata, 1998), pp. 61–62. Political relations soon settled — Castro declared a state of national mourning when his fellow Galician and solider, General Franco, died in 1975 — while many of the Presidents of Spain's democratic period have made state visits to Cuba.

[15] Marisela Fleites-Lear, '¿Victoria contra Corín Tellado?', p. 98.

[16] Germaine Greer, *The Female Eunuch* (London: MacGibbon and Key, 1970), p. 188.

[17] See Duncan Wheeler, 'Raphael and Spanish Popular Song: A Master Entertainer and/or Music for Maids', *Arizona Journal of Hispanic Cultural Studies*, 16 (2012), 11–30.

[18] Dominic Sandbrook, *White Heat: A History of Britain in the Swinging Sixties* (London: Little Brown Company, 2006), p. 410.

reconciliation of personal desire with social imperatives, and the particular form that this takes for women',[19] the author's biography and vast literary output — which span virtually the entirety of the Franco dictatorship (1939–1975), and the subsequent Transition to democracy — are ripe for re-appraisal and non-condescending critical attention.

A Life of Letters: Forging Female Subjectivity during the Dictatorship

A child during the Spanish Civil War (1936–39), Tellado moved from her native Asturias to Cadiz, one of the country's most liberal cities, for a number of years as a teenager. With four brothers and no sisters, she always referred to her adolescent self as something of a tomboy, receiving little attention from the opposite sex, and feeling intimidated by her more glamorous female cousins. As a result of her father's premature death, she had to abandon her studies but her writing soon helped to keep the family afloat. Barely out of her teens when her debut novel, *Atrevida apuesta/Daring Bet* was published in 1947, Tellado became an overnight sensation, the book selling over 750,000 copies in a week.[20]

In the early post-war period, the *novelas rosas* of authors such as María Mercedes Ortoll and Concha Linares Becerra were a ubiquitous presence at a time when books, like food, were frequently in short supply. These were, in many respects, manuals of normative femininity and wish fulfilment frequently construed as correlatives to the instruction of the *Sección Femenina/Women's Section*, a sub-section of the Phalange, the proto-fascist National Movement crucial to the implementation of Francoist doctrine. In fact, as Patricia O'Byrne remarks, '[a]rguably the *novela rosa* was more effective as a subtle instrument of subjugation than the rhetoric of the Sección Femenina, the threat of moral damnation preached by the Church or the regime's repressive legislation which were all more clearly recognizable for what they were'.[21] There was, however, a latent unpredictability inherent in the relationship between text and reader. Hence, for example, the semi-autobiographical narrator in Carmen Martín Gaite's *El cuarto de atrás/The Back Room*, looks back on her adolescence and recalls how she pitied the dictator's daughter, Carmen, because a steady diet of *novelas rosas* accustomed her to imagine all rich heiresses as tearful and ill-treated.[22]

---

[19] Diana Holmes, *Romance and Readership in Twentieth-Century France: Love Stories* (Oxford: Oxford University Press, 2006), p. 18.
[20] Alicia G. Andreu, *La construcción editorial de Corín Tellado*, p. 84.
[21] Patricia O'Byrne, 'Popular Fiction in Post-War Spain: The Smoothing, Subversive *Novela Rosa*', *Journal of Romance Studies*, 8.2 (2008), 37–57 (p. 45).
[22] Carmen Martín Gaite, *El cuarto de atrás* (Barcelona: Destino, 1981), p. 64.

As was the case with many belonging to the higher echelons of the Sección Femenina, Tellado's own biography did not always abide by the establishment script, separating as she did from her husband in 1962. Her novels were simultaneously a continuation of and challenge to the traditional paradigms of both the *novelas rosas* and the times in which she lived. In contrast to the Second Republic (1931–1936), when women's education was greatly expanded, in the early years of the Franco regime very few women had access to university study, and certainly not those like Tellado who were from respectably middle-class but hardly wealthy families. Nevertheless, many of her heroines are graduates and it is tempting to interpret her protagonists' beauty and learning as the projected fantasy of an author who wished she was both more attractive and better educated. Within the context of the time, the mere presence of forthright thinking women was ground-breaking in and of itself, although the novel's endings habitually seek to contain their more radical potentialities.

In *Parecía imposible/It Seemed Impossible*,[23] originally published in 1959, for example, Fred and Diana Cohn could not be more different: he was raised on a ranch in rural America, while she has been educated in France and spends her time with socialites in New York. There is a clash when she first arrives on the ranch, which she half owns, as Fred, an archetypal romance hero,[24] is a non-communicative and unreconstructed male bully to his underlings; as the local priest informs her, there is no softening female presence as he was rejected by a local teacher to whom he made advances. Diana is initially appalled by her cousin's ways, but subsequently falls in love with him as his redemption (as in Delly and indeed many Mills and Boon/Harlequin novels) becomes her mission; she has her first ever kiss after he rescues her on horseback when her life is in danger after she foolishly takes a treacherous route home in adverse weather conditions. A similar but more unsettling narrative from the same year, *La imagen de una mujer/The Image of a Woman*,[25] begins with the tale of two brothers who are heirs to a great American fortune. Whilst his brother squanders his share in Paris by marrying a fickle French woman, Alan is responsible with his inheritance but fails to act on his love for a woman five years his senior. Her dying wish is for him to take care of her daughter, Natalia, as if she were his own. He agrees but goes off in mourning, leaving Natalia in the charge of his sister-in-law, Audrey, and nephew, Jack instructing them to treat her as one of the family. Disregarding his wishes, they treat her as little better than a slave, with Jack even attempting, unsuccessfully, to rape her. Redemption is found when Alan, now in

---

[23] Corín Tellado, *Parecía imposible* (Barcelona: Bruguera, 1979).

[24] Arrogant, powerful and tersely uncommunicative heroes figure for example in Delly's *Esclave ou reine* (*Slave or Queen?*) or *La Biche au bois* (*The Doe in the Forest*), both first published in the early twentieth century but still being re-published in the 1950s and 60s.

[25] Corín Tellado, *La imagen de una mujer* (Barcelona: Bruguera, 1979).

his early thirties, returns, falls in love and marries the teenager who now resembles her mother.

Although many of Tellado's novels were set in Spain, one reason for her frequently transposing the action to abroad might have been that it allowed her to tackle more risqué subject-matter, although the fact that *Ella y su jefe/She and her Boss* features an almost identical narrative to *Los jueves de Leila/Thursdays with Leila* but set in Spain suggests that this argument might have been over-stressed.[26] Although her novels were hardly immune from the censor, a pragmatic approach nevertheless ensured that she became a mistress of ellipsis and, if she pushed things too far, was willing to make adjustments without complaint.

In many cases, however, such measures were unnecessary. *Thursdays with Leila* was passed without objection, the censor commenting that it 'had no message',[27] an ingrained condescension towards the *novela rosa* and female writers as apolitical probably being a more effective camouflage tactic than geographical displacement. In the case at hand, the narrative and characterisation are, for example, predicated on the dire consequences of poverty — a taboo subject when Franco was credited with providing the nation with peace and prosperity — and sexual harassment, an all-too real problem for many young women both in semi-feudal rural Spain and, as the country became a more service-based urban economy, for the office-workers or hotel receptionists who might for the first time be living away from their families. That such issues reappear so incessantly in Tellado's output in the late 1950s and throughout the 1960s suggests that they were more than recurrent literary tropes for at least some of her readers. If in *No te vi/I Didn't See You*,[28] New York secretary Susana makes the decision to wear her hair in a bun and don glasses in order to make herself ugly and therefore be free of unwanted male attention, then the protagonist of *Tu pecado me condena/Your Sin Condemns Me* faces a quandary when her boss makes untoward advances: 'What would happen if she told everyone in Milwaukee who thought Carl Judson was a tireless worker, a decent and humane man, that he had no scruples whatsoever'.[29]

It is a sign not only of the moral perversity of the novels but of the times that narratives are resolved and characters redeemed when the offending male figures genuinely fall in love with the woman and they marry. Reactionary though such denouements may be, they did on occasion introduce a new stock character into Spanish popular fiction: the angelic non-virgin bride. These heroines may have

---

[26] Corín Tellado, *Ella y su jefe* (Barcelona: Bruguera, 1981); Corín Tellado, *Los jueves de Leila* (Barcelona: Bruguera, 1979).

[27] Box No. 3 (50) 21/14167 in the Archivo General de la Administración (Alcalá de Henares).

[28] Corín Tellado, *No te vi* (Barcelona: Bruguera, 1981).

[29] Corín Tellado *Tu pecado me condena* (Madrid: Editorial Rollan, 1968), p. 10. Translation by Duncan Wheeler.

sinned with their bodies, but what was important was that their intentions were pure, with sex frequently construed as a variation on the perennial ideal of female self-abnegation. In *Aventurera/Harlot*, first published in 1963 and set in the English coastal resort of Penzance, the engagement of Mildred and Curk marks the coming together of the town's two most important families. Curk nevertheless starts to have doubts when he strikes up a friendship with Evora, a humble orphan, who he begins to visit on a daily basis, appreciating the warmth of her home which contrasts with what he perceives to be the cold trappings of his wealth and upbringing:

> Evora believed in God and in love. In those two things alone. God came first to her, and then love. And because this love was genuine, she considered it a gift from heaven, never a sin. That's why she loved Curk and admitted him into her home, and she would have accepted an indecent proposal if he had made it. But Curk never had. That was the strange thing. That Curk went to her house every day and never intimated anything like that.[30]

If the sign of his love and respect for her is that he restrains from making sexual advances, her sacrifice is that she is willing for her reputation and future marriage-prospects to be jeopardised by the small-town community assuming she is his mistress. All is, however, resolved, when he plucks up the courage to stand up to his parents, leave his fiancée and marry the woman he genuinely loves.

The parameters of sexual decency are extended in Tellado's novels of this period without ever entirely relinquishing the virgin/whore dichotomy. In *Tengo que abandonarte/I Must Abandon You* (Antonio del Amo, 1969), the only commercially released feature cinematic adaptation of one of her novels and filmed largely in Madrid's National Library, the protagonist is a young female librarian approached on a park bench by an extremely rich man who may look Spanish but is in fact from the Philippines; he is desperate for a son, and proposes they have pre-marital sex in order to see if she can fall pregnant and provide a male heir before he commits to taking her as his wife. She is aghast, until an American friend of his explains the Islamic influence in the Philippines. The prospective groom goes to her home but is seduced by a gold-digging flat-mate. He regrets his actions and marries the more wholesome librarian, reassuring her that she will be happy in the Philippines by explaining that the only member of his family to be Muslim was his great-grandmother, and even she was very beautiful! Once there, however, the young bride is very unhappy as she is unable to fall pregnant. They return to Spain where the lonely and embittered spurned lover blackmails him; his wife drives off in a frenzy, crashing her car. She nearly dies but, on regaining consciousness, the doctor announces mother and

---

[30] Corín Tellado, *Aventurera* (Barcelona: Bruguera, 1979), p. 21. Translation by Duncan Wheeler.

child are both healthy; this is the first that she and her husband know of her pregnancy.

One of the chief contradictions of Tellado's oeuvre is that she rarely left her home, and yet her novels are set all around the world, with detailed descriptions of cities or interiors of hotels into which she had never entered. The epigraphs frequently came from a broad range of sources ranging from the Bible to Flaubert, but most of her reading consisted of newspapers and women's magazines, from which she seemingly gleaned much of her materials and, perhaps, inspiration. As is the case of many autodidacts, the range of her knowledge was impressive but frequently lacking in structure and riddled with basic errors. Spanish customs are frequently transposed in the narratives set in the US: in *Déjanos vivir*,[31] for example, the two protagonists are both shown studying for their *oposiciones* (Spanish state exams for public servants), whilst *Tu pecado me condena* features a *parador*, the Spanish nationalized hotel chain. Alongside the frequent typographical and grammatical errors to be found in early editions of her novels, this sometimes necessitates the translator correcting her work in order not to render it incongruous to the twenty-first century English-language reader. Anachronisms were quite probably rendered invisible to anyone reared on the same cultural diet and national paradigms, at a time when the rapid expansion of the celebrity press was both symptom and cause of a rising consumer culture. Knowledge gleaned from the gossip press imbued Tellado's novels with a hitherto unknown level of detail in terms of her protagonist's leisure activities and possessions that served to make them appear even more realistic, particularly to those many readers whose images of reality came partly from the same sources. In other words, what Justin Crumbaugh terms Spain's 'offbeat rendition of the "happy sixties"',[32] is simultaneously reflected and refracted through Spain's major entry into the pan-European corpus of romance novelists.

Tellado and Romance: *Thursdays with Leila*

Tellado was of a later generation than Britain's Barbara Cartland or France's Delly, but like them she wrote for and enjoyed massive sales in a society tensed between on the one hand the inexorable development of modernity, and on the other a deep-rooted social conservatism. Tellado's tales of love, and of women's difficult quest for material and emotional wellbeing, clearly gave great pleasure to her millions of readers throughout and beyond the Franco years in Spain, as well as in Latin America and, in translation, in other European countries — most notably France and Portugal. Taking *Thursdays with Leila* as our example, what

---

[31] Corín Tellado, *Déjanos vivir* (Barcelona: Bruguera, 1976).
[32] Justin Crumbaugh. *Destination Dictatorship: The Spectacle of Spain's Tourist Boom and the Reinvention of Difference* (Albany: State University of New York Press, 2009), p. 2.

we need to ask is this: where did this pleasure come from? What was it that made millions of readers (ranging, the preface suggests, from domestic workers to educated young women like Vargas Llosa's teenage niece) close the covers of a Tellado novel only to long for the next one? Despite the casual condescension with which the genre is still habitually treated (though there are now very honourable exceptions to this by feminist critics),[33] we can safely assume that fiction readers are neither stupid nor masochistic, and that if so many women have found repeated delight in reading Tellado, it is because there is something there that warrants our attention.

Tellado is a successful practitioner of the well-established genre of popular romantic fiction, and her narrative practice can partly be defined in terms that apply to the genre as a whole. The basic narrative structure at once reflects, dramatizes and in the end pleasurably idealises the pattern of many, even most, of her readers' lives. The heroine starts the story very much alone: Leila, like so many romance heroines, is both orphaned and spatially dislocated, finding herself in a strange town where nothing is familiar. This lends dramatic form to the female experience of entry into adulthood, the need to achieve separation from the mother with whom the girl's identity is often closely entwined, and to find a future beyond the parental home in a world where adult women face restricted options. In the romance as in most women's lives, certainly at the period of Tellado's popularity, the almost inevitable solution to the problems of material and social survival was marriage. The popularity of romance with women readers reflects the extent to which the choice (or imposition) of a male partner has determined women's chances of happiness, and the quality of their lives. But like all good romance heroines, Tellado's Leila is reluctant to acknowledge this, allowing her readers to imagine modes of self-realisation that might not depend on the goodness, charm or otherwise of a husband. Leila is strong, capable, and determined to succeed in her project of making an independent living and taking care of her step-siblings.

Of course He appears, the hero: irresistibly handsome, sexually magnetic, and socially powerful. Stephen Knowles is the alpha male we expect in a romance novel since (at least) Jane Austen's Mr Darcy or Charlotte Bronte's Edward Rochester. His extreme virility is signified — if modestly veiled — by the imagery of hardness and penetration used to characterise him: Stephen is 'harder than stone', his eyes are 'like daggers', 'grey and steely, as cold as knife-blades'. The authority he enjoys is here conferred by birth (he has inherited the family firm), wealth and an imposingly harsh temperament, but can reasonably be said to represent, in amplified form, the reality of male social and sexual power in a deeply patriarchal culture. The vicarious pleasure is thus all the greater — and, one imagines, most

---

[33] See, for example, Janice Radway, *Reading the Romance*.

readers read this precisely in the mode of fantasy — when this harsh exterior turns out to conceal a human heart, accessible only to the heroine whose own extreme sexual charm combined with her resistance to his will unlocks the emotions he has so forcefully repressed. 'And he wasn't an ogre. He was man who perhaps nobody could fathom out, except a woman … a woman who was his'.

Without obstacles to the union between heroine and hero, there is no story: these are provided in classic romance fiction manner chiefly by the hero's own arrogant intransigence and the heroine's refusal to surrender her integrity, but also by their (apparent) differences of social class and degree of wealth. Secondary characters also help to defer the happy ending: a male rival briefly appears in the shape of an honest, respectful engineer who courts Leila, but lacks both the sexual excitement and the potential for narrative conflict of the arrogant alpha male; two minor female characters, Leila's friend Dolly and her rich aunt Marie, demonstrate the risks of remaining a 'spinster'. But the vicarious experience of happiness is offered in the end, albeit in this novel in a form mitigated by the promise of a sequel — for Leila may accept marriage to Stephen as the novel closes, but she has not entirely forgiven him for those shameful 'Thursdays' he has obliged her to undergo.

Thus far, Tellado's success appears to correspond to the success of the romance genre as a whole, and if we are to seek some ethical value in her fiction, despite its apparent endorsement of extreme sexual inequality, this too corresponds to the 'ethic' of the genre. Romantic heroines manage to reconcile emotional and sexual fulfilment (they get their Man) with social acceptance (they achieve wealth and status) by being strong — by refusing to back down on fundamental values. Strength of character is what gets a girl happiness, even if this is always combined with physical beauty (rarely too extreme, to accommodate reader identification of the 'enhanced version of me' type), and even if it always ends up with the dubious reward of marriage to a recently converted tyrant. Popular romance endorses the near-inevitability of marriage, acknowledging its dangers but indulging dreams of it as the road to self-fulfilment: it does not preach female passivity or submission. Beyond this, one might argue too that romance proposes an ideal of relationship that is limited by but could potentially transcend the situation of gendered inequality in which these novels are written. Hero and heroine fall for each other because they are attracted by the other's radical difference from themselves: the work of the narrative is to transform the hero into a partner who can accept the heroine's integrity, whilst maintaining the seductive charm of his 'otherness'. 'The heroine's separate integrity as self is as important to the reader as is the imagined pleasure of that self's unconditional endorsement through love'.[34] Stephen falls in love with Leila because her

---

[34] Diana Holmes, *Romance and Readership*, p. 141.

indifference to material wealth and social status make her radically different from himself; Leila will have to change Stephen if he is to become the kind of man with whom she can be happy, but it is his opacity, the seductive enigma of another consciousness, that attracts her. Even the most 'lowbrow' of romances proposes an ideal of relationship that would combine intense intimacy, founded on reciprocal desire and tenderness, with respect for the other's difference, their uniqueness, their freedom.

Tellado makes effective use of the romance genre, but she also brings to it a particular voice, inflected in part by the context of Franco's Spain. Her heroine, as in most romantic fiction, is at once exceptionally beautiful ('like a film star', 'a head-turner') and a sort of everywoman in her determined ordinariness: 'everyday, nothing fancy' thinks the maid who first focalises Leila for the reader. But in Francoist Spain, conservative and Catholic, ordinary femininity also meant piety — albeit here of a rather vague sort ('whenever she felt depressed she would pray') — and with this went chastity. Not only is it clear, and central to the plot, that any hint of a sexual liaison would dishonour Leila and threaten her future, but she herself feels deeply humiliated by the loss of her virginity, and still more by her own reluctant stirrings of sexual desire. For Tellado's world conforms to the dominant ideology of feminine virtue, probably shared by most of her contemporary readers, and thus eludes the censor, but part of her appeal lies too in the way she acknowledges female sexuality as more than just a bargaining tool for marriage. Chaste as she is, Leila is viscerally affected by Stephen, responding to his presence with deep blushes, 'the mere thought of seeing him' making her 'shiver all over'; reluctantly, she recognises that their illicit Thursday rendezvous represent 'a pernicious pleasure that one somehow still desires'. Tellado's heroines are confirmed in their sense of proper virtue, but also acknowledged as sexual beings.

The social context of Francoist Spain is frequently, as here, transposed to a minimally depicted North American setting. But utterly removed as they are from any aim of social realism, Tellado's novels also acknowledge the harshness of the social climate for a young woman trying to live independently and to forge herself a future. *Thursdays with Leila* is set in the imaginary town of Springfield, a microcosm of what seems to be a world of brutally unregulated capitalism. The firm Stephen owns conforms to no social legislation and acknowledges no workers' rights: it is run according to the whims of its proprietor, which extend to arbitrary dismissal and (as in many other Tellado novels) extreme sexual harassment. To gain a decent education for her half-siblings, Leila must pay high school fees, and the hierarchical nature of health care is crucial to the plot: for her sick half-brother to go to the public hospital, as opposed to an expensive private sanatorium (run as 'a business like any other') would mean his probable death, and it is this dilemma that forces her into her uncomfortable exchange of sex for money. Society imposes strict rules on female behaviour but offers neither material nor legal support to the woman who tries to combine respectability, hence social acceptance, with independence. The magical solution that the genre requires — Leila inherits great wealth after her aunt's deathbed change of heart — resolves but does not negate the depiction of a censorious, hierarchical and profoundly unequal society, one that readers must, at least subliminally, have recognised.

Popular romance aims to cheer the reader, however, rather than simply remind her of life's hardships, and Tellado's counterbalance to the brutality of her heroine's social climate is female friendship, which plays a more prominent role than in, for example, Delly or Cartland. Leila's work colleague Dolly, cheerfully overweight ('tall, broad and fat, her body as big as her heart') and wryly regretful of her single status, warms up the novel with her humour and loyal devotion. Throughout the novel Dolly is an unfailing source of useful information, practical help and irreverent commentary on the arrogant hero, both an ally and a close, sisterly friend. In the background too is the equally faithful Eve, Leila's maid but also a quasi-maternal collaborator in setting up their new home and caring for the children. As the story ends in traditional fashion with the marriage of hero and heroine, neither of these secondary characters is discarded; rather, their presence is represented as crucial to Leila's future happiness, and they will also appear in the sequel volume. Rather than have other women figure as simply rivals or foils to her heroine, Tellado strongly implies the importance of female alliances.

Written at speed, often repetitive or clichéd in style, summary in characterisation, Tellado's fictional world nonetheless *works* by at once mirroring in dramatized form the experience of her readers, and providing enjoyably idealised vicarious resolutions. In its affirmation of female sexuality, its recognition of her society's inhospitality to women's independence, and the role allotted to female solidarity, it brings a quiet note of topical, pre-feminist resistance to the romance script of female solitude, magical meeting, overcoming of obstacles and resolution in marriage. The novel ends with the dilemma of Leila's mingled anger at and love for Stephen unresolved. Focalised by Don Andrés, the priest who has married them, the final scene throws doubt on the possibility of a happy ending: 'Leila loved him. Don Andrés knew that, but ... he also knew that she had been vilely obliged to commit an act that she would regret for the rest of her life, and that nightmare would sour her love in a million different ways'. Thus the hero's moral brutality is not entirely redeemed but has lasting consequences. The text also concludes with Tellado's address to her 'dear readers' cementing the sense of an empathic, hospitable author behind the text, as she invites them to anticipate the pleasure of the sequel and, by implication, of future variations on her narrative of women's survival in a hostile world and their absolute fulfilment in love. These would continue to appear with a regularity that delighted her readers until women's social and political situation came to require a different telling, and a different formulation of the myth of romance.

A Life of Letters 2: Change and Continuity in the Transition to Democracy

Over the course of the 1960s, there is a slight but clearly discernible increase in the range and complexity of vocabulary employed by Tellado. This is probably the symptom of rising standards of literacy, and also the increased availability of the so-called photo-novels adapted from her source texts, first put on the market in 1966 and, by 1968, appearing every fifteen days with an average print-run of 100,000 copies.[35] The highly-popular editions by Rollan publishers of around 60 pages featured actors photographed in a range of, admittedly limited, settings and used the kind of speech bubbles typical of comics of the period. The highest sales for these were registered in Andalusia and Galicia alongside the poor neighbourhoods of Barcelona and Madrid filled with rural emigrants,[36] areas where literacy rates remained low and the much-heralded miracles of modernity remained largely off-limits.

In the manner of a film poster, the opening page advertised the actors who would appear in an adaptation of a Tellado novel. There was a veritable star-system with Conchita Cura and Juan M. Solano being repeatedly paired and photographed as a youthful couple; back pages were frequently dedicated to advertisements for up-coming adaptations of novels by Tellado, or other romantic novelists of the day. On the back-cover to the photo-novel of *Me obligaron a dejarte/They Made Me Leave You*, for example, there is an announcement of a new major series titled *Cuerpos y almas/Bodies and Souls* sold in the following terms:

> Bodies that suffer and souls that experience stories imbued with a passionate realism designed just for you. Doctors and nurses fighting against pain and death brought to life by your favourite protagonists from the Corín Tellado, Selene and Embelseco series together for the first time to make you tremble with the most passionate and marvellous stories imaginable.[37]

The format, content and readership of the photo-novel were, somewhat predictably, held up to ridicule. The cover of the 1971 edition of Juan Goytisolo's *Fin de fiesta/End of the Party* — first published in 1962 and comprising four tales of relationship strife, set against the backdrop of the increasingly multicultural Spanish coastline — features a front cover that self-consciously parodies the kind of imagery employed by the photo-novels, which now formed the cultural diet of women represented in the novel by the mother of the male protagonist, a woman as obsessed by the arrival of tourists and their money as by reports of the

---

[35] Juan Miguel Sánchez Vigil and María Olivera Zaldua 'La fotografía en las fotonovelas españolas', *Documentación de las Ciencias de la Información*, 35 (2012), 31–51 (p. 36).
[36] Ángeles Carmona González, *Corín Tellado*, pp. 156–57.
[37] Corín Tellado, *Fotonovela: Me obligaron a dejarte* (Madrid: Editorial Rollan, 1971), p. 60. Translation by Duncan Wheeler.

Shah's wife's forthcoming trip to the Costa del Sol.[38] As in much of his work, Goytisolo construes the consumerist culture of late Francoism to be a grotesque hybrid of dictatorial control, mass-media manipulation and capitalist perversion.

For better or worse, the arrival of mass tourism alongside an expanding middle class and an increasingly consumerist society ensured the Transition was relatively peaceful, with the apparatus of dictatorship gradually dismantled from within as Spain transformed itself into a liberal monarchical democracy, and modes of conduct and relationships became increasingly European. Almost completely bypassing the grand political narratives of the time, Tellado's novels nevertheless provided an on-going commentary on changing socio-cultural mores. As María Teresa González García notes:

> It was from 1976 onwards that Tellado introduced in her novels sexual relationships outside marriage, featuring mainly a despondent husband looking for consolation in his lovers' arms. The novelist warned her female readers that infidelity was a dangerous game for them to play. The crime of adultery committed by women was finally removed from the Spanish Legal Code on 19 February 1978 and two months later Tellado published *Cuéntame qué pasa* [Tell Me What's Happening], in which a child is born of an adulterous relationship.[39]

In-keeping with the fashion of the time, Tellado even began to write erotic novels under the pseudonym of Ada Miller.

There was a veritable boom in narratives of generational conflict at the time, most profitably exploited by the cloying nostalgic revisionism of the best-selling novels of Fernando Vizcaíno Casas. Many ordinary Spaniards were particularly concerned about the generational gap: according to a government sociological study from 1980, arguments about how to bring up and educate children were by far the chief source of conflict and dispute between partners.[40] If, over the preceding decades, Tellado's youthful protagonists had become gradually older, albeit not at the same rate as the author, her novels from the Transition return incessantly to the clashes between parents and children who, her novels suggest, frequently lack a common language.

The eponymous protagonist of *El caso de Sandra/Sandra's Case* is a mother and doctor who has defied her family by leaving her husband who had been her first love but had sabotaged their marriage through a combination of controlling

---

[38] Juan Goytisolo, *Fin de fiesta* (Barcelona: Seix Barral, 1971).
[39] María Teresa González García, 'The Evolution of Women in Spanish Society During the Second Half of the Twentieth Century According to a Populist Novelist: Corín Tellado', in *A Rich Field Full of Pleasant Surprises: Essays on Contemporary Literature in Honour of Professor Socorro Suárez Lafuente*, ed. by José Francisco Fernández and Alejandra Moreno Álvarez (Newcastle: Cambridge Scholars Publishing, 2014), pp. 167–83 (p. 182).
[40] Centro de Investigaciones Sociológicas, *Pareja humana: Estudio No 1.234* (Madrid: Centro de Investigaciones Sociológicas, 1980).

jealousy and lack of ambition.[41] Setting up a new business in a provincial town, the twenty-something single mother finds romance in the guise of a sociology graduate she hires to look after her son and take care of her domestic affairs. In *No quiero ser falso/I Don't Want to be False*, a young female graduate who has found work in a bingo hall — public gambling was decriminalised in Spain in 1977, with bingo rapidly establishing itself as a metonym for sophistication and modernity difficult to imagine in most Anglo-American contexts — commences an affair with a married pilot who only wed at the age of eighteen to avoid a scandal when his sixteen year old girlfriend fell pregnant. His new lover faces a quandary:

> She didn't know what arguments to wield in order to make her parents aware
> of the situation. They weren't bad people, just old fashioned, they'd never
> moved with the times and thought the same way they had forty years
> previously ... She could easily fall victim to their intransigence.[42]

Tellado's novels perform a pedagogical role in preparing her readership for the onset of democracy and new values albeit within certain circumscribed limits.

In *Voy a vivir con él/I'm Going to Live with Him*, the protagonist is Ana, a twenty-three year old virgin who has taken her mother's surname because she is trying to make it in television but does not want to rely on the reputation of her father, a renowned filmmaker. She rejects various suitors out of a fear of ending up like her own mother or the wives of her male colleagues; in her own words: 'I am not a militant feminist or a man-hater, but I am committed to the idea that women are more than just baby-making machines'.[43] In the end, however, she falls in love but this is not seen to be the end of her professional career: 'He would continue to run an agency and she would work as a film director ... But, above all else, they were a man and a woman, and they were going to enjoy each other'.[44]

If Tellado's ideal female heroine is a physically attractive educated woman capable of loving and being loved, her male protagonists can seemingly be redeemed and forgiven any failing apart from the inability to love, a facet considered far more important than good looks and given explicit narrative emphasis from the 1970s onwards. In *No me mires así/Don't Look at Me Like That*, Charles is the very attractive singer of a Belgian rock and roll band but the novel suggests that he is not good enough for the heroine, Nell, because he is unmanly; this is signified through references to a traumatised childhood and to his repeated handwashing in what would now be understood as a symptom of

---

[41] Corín Tellado, *El caso de Sandra* (Barcelona: Libros y publicaciones, 1984).
[42] Corín Tellado, *No quiero ser falso* (Barcelona: Bruguera, 1983), p. 15. Translation by Duncan Wheeler.
[43] Corín Tellado, *Voy a vivir con él* (Barcelona: Bruguera, 1979), p. 17. Translation by Duncan Wheeler.
[44] Ibid., p. 94. Translation by Duncan Wheeler.

OCD.[45] Conversely, the heroic César from *Hay algo que se muere/Something is Dying* is described as follows: 'He wasn't an Adonis by any stretch of the imagination. But he was a man. A man through and through as Unamuno would say'.[46] This dichotomy is brought out with a particular lack of subtlety in *Quiero a tu mujer/I Love Your Wife* in which Sandra rejects Álvaro in favour of his best friend, the physically enticing José.[47] The former tries to convince her against marriage with the latter not out of jealousy but because he knows from a prostitute that José is impotent; a physical ailment is seen to be the symptom and cause of a moral and spiritual perversity that, ultimately, will lead Sandra into Álvaro's arms. A happy ending is provided by the unsatisfied wife receiving a medical certificate confirming her virginity that is used to shame José and annul the marriage, paving the way for a sexually satisfying union between the less attractive but more virile male and his bride.

Tellado's relative modernity and compassion were frequently disregarded at a time when she increasingly became the source of exclusion and ridicule. Her daughter Begoña, for example, recalls bitterly experiences of being mocked by lecturers in front of her peers while studying for a degree in journalism at Madrid's Complutense University.[48] Although it would have been more radical to explore the sexual fantasies of middle-aged female protagonists raised under Franco (as Rosa Montero would in *Te trataré como una reina/I'll Treat you Like a Queen*),[49] Tellado does go some way to making legible the voice and values of a new generation of women in a more compassionate and less condescending manner than the caricatures of demonic pious mothers who would subsequently became a staple of best-selling and frequently erotically-charged novels written by female novelists who came of age during the Transition, such as *Las edades de Lulú/The Ages of Lulu* by Almudena Grandes or *Beatriz y los cuerpos celestes/Beatriz and the Heavenly Bodies* by Lucía Etxebarría.[50]

Conversely, however, Tellado's novels frequently seem to want to have it both ways: to salaciously depict new mores without renouncing the moral certainties of yesteryear. *Fin de Semana/Weekend*, first published in 1984, for example, details the amorous adventures of Anita and Débora who meet as teenagers on a plane from Madrid to London where they lose their virginity, a prelude to picking up numerous Adonis-like new lovers and languages as they travel around Europe,

---

[45] Corín Tellado, *No me mires así* (Barcelona: Bruguera, 1983).

[46] Corín Tellado, *Hay algo que su muere* (Barcelona: Bruguera, 1976), p. 40. Translation by Duncan Wheeler.

[47] Corín Tellado, *Dos apasionantes relatos de amor para tú: Quiero a tu mujer y Una chica especial* (Bracelona: Libros y Publicaciones Periódicas, 1984).

[48] Anecdote recounted to Duncan Wheeler.

[49] Rosa Montero, *Te trataré como a una reina* (Barcelona: Seix Barral, 2012).

[50] Almudena Grandes *Las edades de Lulú* (Barcelona: Fábula Tusquets, 2004); Lucía Etxebarría, *Beatriz y los cuerpos celestes* (Barcelona: Destino, 2009).

before settling down with life-partners in Spain. Anita summarises the situation to her friend as follows: 'Deep down we are still Spanish women and pure ones at that. We have purity of the soul, which is the true purity, whilst we have learned something from every experience, which is important when it comes to choosing a husband'.[51] If the first half of the novel is depicted through the third-person omniscient narrator that is the default mode of storytelling for almost all of Tellado's novels, then the second half is rendered through letters the two friends send to each other.

This is symptomatic of Tellado experimenting with both content and form in the late 1970s and 1980s. *Orientación Femenina/Feminine Orientation* is a first-person narration about a female lawyer, who establishes a firm for the many women suffering domestic abuse or victims of rape; she continues with this social and professional endeavour even after falling in love and settling down with a married man who is unsatisfied by his superficial uneducated wife and who, when he attempts to find relief through prostitutes, is so disgusted with them and himself that he returns home to read Cervantes' *Don Quixote*![52] As Spain became more democratic and culture became a supreme fetish — wonderfully parodied by the spoof television show "Hay que leer más"/"You Must Read More" in Pedro Almodóvar's film *Kika* (1993) — Tellado was nevertheless seen to be an increasingly anachronistic figure, a historical curiosity at best. By the onset of the 1980s, she was a far more significant cultural phenomenon in many Latin American countries than at home. As was the case with many icons of Francoist popular culture, she found a ready audience in Pinochet's Chile, where she was treated as a visiting dignitary on her arrival in 1981 by a dictator who had been the only major world-leader to attend General Franco's funeral. It is symptomatic of certain structural and cultural parallels between the two dictatorships that, in 1990, Chilean television produced a series of twenty-plus episodes based on her most emblematic novels.

Tellado had periodically had legal and personal battles with her publishers Bruguera, but had always returned to the stable despite being aware that her labour was being exploited. The master of the kiosks nevertheless went bankrupt in 1986. Spain was changing and, once Harlequin established a Hispanic subsidiary with great success in the late 1970s, Tellado would never again enjoy such a monopoly on either the romantic publishing market or the imaginations of millions of Spanish women.[53] This did not, however, prevent the author from continuing to produce novels, providing her readers with a bespoke depiction of the outside world that she continued to observe from a provincial room of her

---

[51] Corín Tellado, *Fin de semana* (Madrid: Suma de Letras, 2005), p. 48. Translation by Duncan Wheeler.

[52] Corín Tellado, *Orientación femenina* (Barcelona: Libros y publicaciones, 1984).

[53] Chris Perriam, Michael Thompson, Susan Frenk and Vanessa Knights, *A New History of Spanish Writing 1939 to the 1990s* (Oxford: Oxford University Press, 2000), p. 188.

own at a time when, as Mario Vargas Llosa recalls, she lived in constant fear because she had refused to give money demanded of her by ETA or, perhaps more likely, common criminals masquerading as members of the Basque terrorist organisation.[54] In *Prejuicios raciales/Racial Prejudices*, the beautiful Mag Castillo plans to leave her studies to marry her boyfriend, Ignacio, who unceremoniously dumps her when his parents inform him that his fiancée was adopted and is the biological daughter of gypsies: "'[…] they were willing to accept my friendship with your adopted parents, but me getting together with a gypsy girl was no laughing matter. Gypsies are a hateful race, I've always disliked them'".[55] Karma and role reversal comes into play when Mag qualifies as a doctor and a recently impoverished Ignacio has to beg for her charity and compassion on discovering his father has cancer; although the novel is at pains to observe that the state now provides excellent public health services, old habits die hard and it is unthinkable for this family who made their fortune under the dictatorship to receive anything other than what they perceive to be the best medical attention.

La revelación de Sue/Sue's Revelation, one of the most reprinted of her later works, even daringly (if somewhat clumsily) introduces the possibility of same-sex romance.[56] The novel opens with a quote from Montaigne before transporting the reader to a seedy world of glamour photography in Los Angeles. Patrick runs the business alongside the butch Sue, replete with hairy legs, who rebuffs any male advances but is very protective of Sandra, a beautiful model who was sexually abused as a child. Sue's business partner realises she is in love and together they come up with a ruse by which she will disappear and reappear as Brian, reputedly Sue's cousin; the strategy works and Brian seduces Sandra almost instantaneously. Byzantine, sensational and frankly bizarre narratives of this kind were not without their readers, but Tellado no longer had the same grip on global popular culture as she had decades previously when millions of women devoured narratives such as *Los jueves de Leila* in a way that is almost impossible to recreate in the present. Tellado's decades-long success is both a symptom and cause of the fact that, in Spain as in most Western nations, fiction readers are more female than male, with literature the one cultural activity — at least according to predominantly male sociologists — to be dominated by women.[57] The novel translated here dates from the heyday of Tellado's popularity, and exemplifies the slapdash style and narrative verve, piety and subversion, timeless myth and topicality that made Tellado queen of the Spanish romance.

---

[54] Anecdote told by Mario Vargas Llosa to Duncan Wheeler.

[55] Corín Tellado, *2 apasionantes relatos de amor para tu corazón: Sublime situación y Prejuicios raciales* (Barcelona: libros y Publicaciones Periódicas, 1984), p. 29. Translation by Duncan Wheeler.

[56] Corín Tellado, *La revelación de Sue* (Barcelona: Bruguera, 1982).

[57] Enrique Gil Calvo, *La era de las lectoras: el cambio cultural de las mujeres españolas* (Madrid: Instituto de la Mujer and Ministerio de Asuntos Exteriores, 1993), p. 42.

Thursdays with Leila

by
Corín Tellado

Translated by
Duncan Wheeler

CHAPTER I

"My name is Leila Heimer. I am here to see Miss Heimer."

The young woman looked the visitor up and down curiously. Leila Heimer. Could it be her mistress's daughter, a niece perhaps?

"Come in. I will find out if Miss Heimer is available. Miss Heimer lets me know every morning if she's expecting visitors. She hasn't mentioned anyone today."

"I'm her niece."

The young woman smiled. Her curiosity was satisfied. She was very pretty, her mistress' niece. Very pretty, and very … personable? Yes, perhaps. Her grey eyes maintained a steady gaze. Her smooth forehead rose softly, without the slightest hint of arrogance. The maid's scorching eyes looked down at the visitor's clothes. Everyday, nothing fancy. Her mistress was a millionaire. How could it be that her niece paid a visit dressed in a fashion that could almost be described as down at heel. There were better clothes to be found in her own humble wardrobe than those worn by Miss Heimer's niece. A simple skirt made with cheap wool, a knitted cardigan whose colour had long faded, flat shoes and an old-fashioned handbag.

"Are you going to tell Miss Heimer I'm here or not?"

"Oh, yes. Right away!"

She left with haste, almost running. Leila looked around and a sarcastic smile extended across her face. Marie Heimer was a wealthy lady, perhaps amongst the wealthiest in Springfield. By contrast, she and her siblings …?

She shrugged her shoulders. At the end of the day, so what? She didn't envy her aunt's wealth. Neither had she gone there looking for a hand-out. She saw it as a duty to pay her a visit, and Leila was doing it because she always made sure to fulfil her obligations.

"Go right ahead, Miss Heimer." Leila was taken aback by the young woman's high pitched voice. She looked towards the maid, who indicated where to go and followed in silence. The mansion was huge, full of works of art, pictures, sculptures, carpets … Her lips curled into a soft smile. With no conscious effort to conjure the image, she recalled the room she had shared with her siblings in New York up to now. Leila was also reminded of her mother, who had died some four years previously. All those years of toil to die so pointlessly on a charity ward. She closed her eyes.

"This way. Go right ahead." And, with a nasal voice, she announced, "Miss Heimer."

The maid entered, with Leila following. She found herself in a grand living space, with a carpet as thick as a wall. Original paintings by famous artists. Translucent porcelain ornaments. A fireplace at the far end. A sofa, three armchairs; Marie Heimer was to be found immersed in one of them. She was a tall lady, with blonde hair, stick-thin with an arrogant and cold demeanour. An intimidating figure just to look at. Leila was not, however, overwhelmed. She knew her aunt already, and had seen her on two prior occasions. First, when her father had died and, then, when her mother had remarried.

"Come in," beckoned the lady without making any movement. At her side was a dog the size of a pony with luxuriant fur. It was asleep at Marie's feet and, under its snout, there lay a bronze dish filled with pastries. Leila's lips curved, making a strange gesture. That dog scorned its pastries. And her siblings didn't have food on their plates ... It was despicable, but she had no intention of reproaching her for it. She hadn't gone there to berate her aunt.

"I said, come in." The old maid was getting impatient as if she'd seen Leila yesterday.

It had been years. How many? Who knows, but it had been an age since they had seen each other. Leila moved towards her with resolve, retaining composure as she stood in front of the huge arm-chair.

"Sit yourself down," Marie invited, with a condescending smile. "You've grown a lot since the last time I saw you."

"It's been thirteen years," she replied serenely. "I'm now twenty-two years old."

"That's true. I'm not accustomed to keeping track of the years." She idly caressed the dog's back. "I told you to sit down. It's a miracle you turning up here. Have you been thrown off your high horse?"

Leila sat down and crossed her legs naturally. "I was never on a high horse," she said dryly. "And, even if I had been, I've not come here to argue about it."

"I didn't ask you to come," the millionairess clarified coldly.

"True enough. But I'm accustomed to doing my duty."

"Duty? And what duty compelled you to pay me a visit that I neither requested nor want?"

"Your charitable nature and good will does you credit."

"Leila, I don't think you've come here to judge me. And bear in mind that I won't allow it."

"Nor would I take that liberty."

"I admire your common sense."

"It's not something I've ever lacked."

"Have you come here to tell me that?" she asked, putting an end to the play on words with a cool cold gesture.

"Of course not."

"I thought you were all in New York. I don't suppose you will force me to endure the humiliation of seeing those three bastards here."

"Hold your insults right there," she exclaimed, hardly able to repress her indignation. "They are my brother and sisters, and I love them."

"You've always been prone to sentimentality."

"I'm proud of the fact."

"Like your father, that idiot brother of mine."

"You shouldn't speak ill of the dead, Aunt Marie," she said, struggling to get the words out. "Your brother was a great man."

"Yes, of course," the lady scornfully laughed, caressing the giant dog's back again. "That is until he lost his mind and married a woman in my service."

"She was a woman who made him happy."

"Right. But she didn't have any qualms about remarrying. Why have you come?" she asked without the slightest hint of warmth.

"I was working in an important company in New York."

"Yes," she interrupted her. "I know. Since your mother died, you've turned yourself into Theresa of Calcutta for those three leper siblings of yours."

"Aunt Marie!"

"Alright, I apologise if I've offended you, young lady. As far as I'm concerned those three siblings of yours will always be three mongrels. What I can't fathom is why you have taken charge of them and refused to come and live with me."

"Because I don't love you and I adore them. Because you didn't need me, and without me they would have died. Because …"

"Alight, that's quite enough. Tell me once and for all why you've come, and then clear off. My nerves are all over the place, and your mere presence unsettles me."

"I'll be out of your hair soon enough. The company went bust. I found myself without work, and last week they offered me a job in an automobile business around here. In the offices if you know what I mean. I've come to work in Springfield, and I thought I had the duty to pay you a visit. That's all." She stood up. "I won't bother you again."

"And you've got the nerve to tell me you're coming to Springfield to work. You, my niece. Do you think I'm going to stand for it?"

"Don't worry, Aunt Marie. This visit is pure protocol. Nobody will find out I'm the daughter of your brother."

"But I'll know, you foolish girl."

"I'm sorry, Aunt Marie," she replied with dignity. "There wasn't any work for me in New York. We're not going to die of hunger just because you want us to."

"You've always had a place at my side," the lady shouted out, beginning to lose her composure. "I came to seek you out when your father died."

"But you didn't offer my mother shelter, Aunt Marie. And she … was my mother. You would have realised what that meant, if you had had kids."

"Get out!" she screamed, losing her composure completely. "And make sure not to come back."

"I swear," she said heading for the door. "And I can also assure you I won't acknowledge you if I see you in the street. You have my word."

"Get out!"

"Goodbye."

* * *

The flat the factory provided for her was small, but sufficient for the four of them and Eve, the maid, who never abandoned them. Living quarters comprised four bedrooms, a kitchen, bathroom and dining room. The factory offered them money for furniture in exchange for docking six dollars a week from her wage. She earned forty a week, so that left thirty-four for food, clothes and to pay for her siblings' education. Leila didn't have any savings, and she thought life was cruel but she didn't lose hope. She was a patient young woman, who faced life with resignation. Often she would recall her mother's sweet phrases: "Don't ever despair in the face of the Lord's ways. He who inflicts the wound will provide the remedy." In reality, that was the way things were. However bad things got, there was always some refuge where she could take solace. Whenever she felt depressed, she would pray and a new flame of hope would emerge from within. Then peace and a sense that things were put right, even if she would later be assailed by that sense of desperation yet again.

Eve and she bought the furniture. They turned the flat into a cosy nest carved out of the tenderness that had never been absent from the Heimer's humble abode. They furnished three bedrooms. Eve slept in one, with Martha next to her in a Z-bed. She was a happy ten-year old girl. Another bedroom was for Rob, who was twelve years old, and already knew what it meant to have a sense of responsibility. And the other one was for her. Her bed was wide and seven-year old Gladys slept at her side.

They turned a little room into a kind of play-room for the kids and set up a simple but welcoming dining room. Leila's exquisite feminine touch shone through in even the smallest details, that strong personality which she hid from others and revealed to herself alone.

She began to work. Thank God the flat was a long way from the residential avenue on which her aunt lived. And, in any case, Leila didn't have sufficient funds for a social life, and there was no fear of bumping into her aunt. She wasn't afraid of work. The only thing to worry her was her siblings' studies. Martha was preparing to start high school, with Rob already in the second year. Her salary didn't stretch to covering their tuition fees. Eve did wonders in the kitchen but, for all the maid's efforts and Leila's work, the household budget could only go so far. And it wasn't sufficient.

One day, she decided to visit the office manager. She explained her situation, not asking for a salary raise, but more work. They supplied her with a typewriter and she worked from home. She felt something close to happiness. Having doubled her salary within a month, she could rest easy once she had been able to secure Rob and Martha places in a fee-paying school. Brother and sister came home for lunch and, sometimes, in the evenings, after doing his homework, Rob would help her with the copies she had to type.

Life in this way unfolded in their humble, calm and quiet abode. She would dedicate an hour a day to teaching Gladys to read. Clever and diligent like Rob and Martha, the young girl learnt quickly.

One morning, on arriving at the office, her workmate Dolly whispered to her: "Watch your back, the boss is coming in today."

Leila was taken aback. "The boss? When did he go away? I saw him yesterday afternoon."

"Bah," said Dolly dismissively. "You're talking about the office manager. There are twenty departments in this building, each with their own manager. I'm talking about the boss of everything. The head honcho so to speak."

"Oh! I thought the factory belonged to a group of shareholders."

"Well you got that wrong. It is the exclusive property of one Mister Stephen Knowlton."

"Oh!"

"And he's not the type to take it easy in his prince's palace. He's the type to work all night, the first to arrive in the morning."

"Well, it's the first I've heard of him."

"Yes, he's been away travelling."

"I get it. But I doubt he'll bother nosing around here."

"That all depends. He's a strange guy. Harder than stone, with a heart like meat past its sell by date."

"Hardly a flattering comparison."

"No more than he deserves. He doesn't take pity on anyone, you know. He's got eyes that see right through you. He's blonde, with eyes like daggers."

"Married?"

"Of course not. Nobody's got a chance with him. Everyone knows how hard he is by nature, with his heart of stone," she laughed maliciously. "Because it doesn't feel a thing, you know. I don't think he'd take pity even on his own mother. And he's got one. A lady who goes about the place in a white car, always sat next to some ancient old woman, almost like a lady-in-waiting who keeps her company."

"And does she drive the car?" asked Leila, taken aback.

"No, sweetie. A chauffeur drives; he's very stiff, dresses in blue with a gold sash. I'm telling you this because everybody in Springfield knows that white car, her lady in waiting and the chauffeur. Also, for your information, she's very charitable."

"Who does the nasty son take after then?"

"I don't know. His father, our old boss, was a true gentleman."

"Is he young?"

"Yes, of course. He must be about thirty, although he looks older. Also, so you know, he's very elegant and well-dressed. All the eligible girls in Springfield, the heiresses I mean, throw themselves at his feet but it looks as if he's got the measure of all of them, despising them as much as I do."

"And he's never looked at you?" asked Leila, enjoying the exchange.

"At me? As if, when he doesn't look at anyone apart from to grunt or groan. He only looks down at people. You'll meet him soon enough."

"That's if I do meet him. Maybe I won't."

"That's what you think. The second he enters the office, they bring him up-to-speed on the employees. He then summons anyone who's new and, one by one, passes judgement on them. It wouldn't be the first time he's fired someone without providing any kind of explanation."

"Heavens above! Might he fire me?" she shuddered.

"Try and respond respectfully and with submission to everything he asks. He hates anyone as haughty as he is. A question of principle," she laughed.

Leila bowed her head towards the typewriter, and set to work, a frown on her face.

CHAPTER II

It wasn't difficult to spot that the atmosphere had changed in all the different departments. Their managers spoke through gestures, and seemed nervous. Mister Leigh, Leila's boss, was ill at ease. When Dolly and Leila left at the end of the day, they looked at each other and Dolly commented, mockingly: "I've been working for the Knowltons for six years. There was a sense of community when the father was alive. Then he died and the whole place was put on edge. Don't profits need to go up? Yes, of course, but not at the expense of us being put down and threatened, with the threat of being fired always hanging over us."

"There must be a union that'll defend our interests," objected Leila.

"Yes, of course. But that doesn't worry the heartless Mister Knowlton in the slightest. When he decides to fire an employee, he always lets the union know first, pays a settlement and that's the end of that. Bear in mind that he's the richest man in Springfield. The city has one hundred and sixty three thousand people living in it and, with the exception of Miss Heimer, the owner of the paper and textile factory, nobody's in a position to stand up to him. That's how it is," she added, as if to remind herself. "By the way, are you related in any way to that ridiculous Lady?"

Leila said no with a shake of the head.

"I just asked because of the surname."

"It's a common name."

"That's true. What was I saying?"

"We were talking about the union and Mister Knowlton."

"Ah, yes! The union bosses are his mates and a man with that much money inspires fear, and they try not to contradict him."

"I'm thinking, Dolly. What would happen if he found out Mister Leigh gives me work to do at home?"

"Um. I fear he'd have a real go at him, and make sure he stopped giving it to you."

"Doesn't he ever take pity on his fellow-man?"

"Not in the least. He wouldn't know pity if it slapped him about the face. Those who knew him as a kid say he abused his dogs and birds, and that his parents could never control him. But he had an incredible mind for business. Since he's been in charge of the company, everything has run like clockwork, and profits have doubled. I guess," added Dolly, switching subject as was her wont, "that you won't eat at home. Shall we go into this cafe?"

"My brother and sisters …"

"You need to learn to live for yourself a bit."

"Dolly. I live only for them."

"Alright, but you shouldn't forget about yourself." And, looking her up and down: "Forgive me for poking my nose into your private life, but I'm very fond of you. I've never met a girl like you before, and I'm really pleased to have you as a workmate."

"Thanks."

Dolly raised her shoulders, and added affectionately: "It's great that you work for your brother and sisters. It's awful to have to look after three siblings with no money. I, thank the Lord, don't have any relatives. It means I don't have to worry about everyday family problems."

"I adore my brother and sisters," Leila abruptly interrupted her.

"I'm not criticising you, my dear. Perhaps, in your situation, I would have felt the same, but that doesn't mean you can't look out for yourself. You are," she added quickly, not giving Leila the chance to object, "a beautiful young woman. As you can see, I'm thirty already. I've wasted the best years of my life without anyone telling me what beautiful eyes I have." Without bitterness, she started to laugh. "If truth be told, it doesn't bother me too much. In all fairness, I never had beautiful eyes so I can't blind men with my beauty. But you, heaven's above, you're like a film-star."

"Dolly, don't mock me. You're very hard on yourself, and almost merciless with me."

"I'm being fair and reasonable. You should dress better. How about we go shopping after-work?"

"Dolly, you know I can't. I don't have any money."

"I'll lend it to you."

"But why are you taking such an interest?"

"Because I don't want you to waste your youth like I wasted mine. It's the only thing that, once lost, can never be found again. And I don't imagine you want to wind up an old maid?"

"How do I know?"

"It's fine that you sacrifice some things for your three siblings, but I think it's weird that you give yourself up completely for them."

"Let's drop the subject, Dolly. I'll join you for lunch, but on the condition that you avoid bringing this up again."

"Deal, on the condition that you accept my loan, and the two of us go shopping this evening."

"No."

"Just like that, without leaving any room for discussion."

"Forgive me."

"You're too lofty," grumbled Dolly, who enjoyed getting the best out of the beauty of youth, which she had never had.

"I promise I'll take care of myself," said Leila tenderly. "But with my money."
Dolly started to laugh and remarked, "You're so proud."

* * *

"Miss Leila …" She thought to herself, my time's up. Last in, first out. I was hired because of a recommendation, and it'll be me who will be fired. She suddenly shuddered.

"Can you come into my office for a second, Miss Leila?" the office manager asked again. Leila looked at Dolly, whose eyes said, "Be brave. Go in. Face up to whatever and don't be cowed by anything."

"Right away, Mister Leigh." And she went into his office. He had left the door open. The intercom over which she had been called hadn't been switched off.

"Come in and sit down," invited the avuncular Mister Leigh and, with a kind voice, for he was aware of Leila's situation at home, he added: "Don't be scared. Nothing serious is going to happen. Sit down, please."

She sat down at the edge of a big seat, facing Mister Leigh's window. He looked at her for a second: "Miss Leila," he began, "you started to work here because I received a letter of recommendation."

"Yes, precisely, Mister Leigh."

"Your position in these offices is secure."

"They won't fire me?"

A satisfied smile spread across the boss's lean face. "Of course not, Miss Leila; but … I'm not going to be able to give you work to take home. It goes against company policy."

"That work's the only thing that allows me to pay for my siblings' education," Leila said calmly. "And that's really important to me."

"I know. As you are aware, Mister Knowlton arrived yesterday morning. I offered you work under my watch. Once here, all of us managers are summoned to see him and to account for what we've been up to. He's against the decision I've taken, and has ordered me to stop any overtime. In this company, there's sufficient staff to carry out all the work that needs doing during normal office hours. I have an explicit order from Mister Knowlton to hire more people if and when it's required, but, as I've already said, the same order prohibits overtime. Here's the memo I've just received from above."

"You are very kind, Mister Leigh."

"You came recommended by my brother, and that's enough in my book. You worked with my brother until the firm went bust. I have excellent personal references for you. And, because of that," he added affectionately, "I've taken the liberty of talking to a friend, who will give you work to do at home. It's easy and comfortable work. Addressing envelopes; he'll pay a cent for every one done."

"That's a lot," she said, taken aback.

"Yes. But you won't have an unlimited number of envelopes. There will be a set number each week."

"In any case, it'll be a great help at home."

"That's why I decided to speak to him on your behalf."

"I don't know how I can pay you back."

"Don't mention it. You can return to your desk now."

"Thanks, Mister Leigh."

She recounted what had taken place to Dolly, who replied: "The ogre came back. It's the same every year. What I still can't work out is how Mister Knowlton doesn't realise they take advantage of the months he's away to make up with generous deeds the good will he withholds during the rest of the year."

"Is he really as hard as he seems?"

"Worse than you can imagine."

"Listen, I've been thinking … You don't think he's had his heart broken?"

Dolly started to laugh and stifled her guffaw with her two hands. "A guy like that having his heart broken?" She turned towards her workmate's desk and, with complicity, added: "I can't imagine Stephen, the little angel, kissing and falling in love with a woman."

"But, at the end of the day, he's a man like all the rest."

"He's more than that," mocked Dolly, "because he has more money, but as far as women are concerned … You make me laugh! I don't think that maniac would be capable of telling a girl he loved her, and the idea of him kissing a sweetheart seems even more ridiculous. He's better suited to slapping than caressing."

"You make him sound like a monster."

"That's exactly what he is. A monster with a silver spoon, extraordinary, formidable, a blank cheque made flesh, you can put whatever quantity you want, without fear that the account will run out, but a human monster nonetheless."

"I have no desire to meet him."

At that very moment, a mechanical female voice announced over the intercom: "Miss Leila Heimer to the chief executive's office."

Leila stood to attention without thinking, and Dolly smiled with amusement. "There you go," Dolly said quietly. "You're going to meet him. Put your armour on." Leila went out, pale as a ghost.

* * *

The door opened automatically for her. Leila relaxed straight away. At the far end there was a boardroom table, and behind that a blond muscular man dressed in black. Immersed in a thick book, he seemed unaware the door had been opened. Three women were rushing back and forth with papers, books, envelopes … There was also a young man, who Leila recognised straight away as the bellboy from the first floor.

"Good afternoon," she greeted. The three women responded, but the blonde man remained oblivious to her presence. His eyes were hidden behind gold-rimmed tinted glasses and, every so often, he put his fingers between the frame and his eyes before removing them to turn the pages in his book.

"Mister Knowlton," said one of the secretaries. "Miss Leila Heimer is here." He didn't answer. The secretary must have been accustomed to silent responses, because she turned back to Leila and, in a friendly fashion, said: "If you'd be as kind as to take a seat." She indicated a seat in front of the table, where the man continued to be oblivious to everything. Leila tightened her fists. He had a solitary air about him. The minutes passed by: five, ten, a quarter of an hour. She observed Mister Knowlton on the other side of the desk. He responded to three phone-calls in that fifteen minutes, asked for a file, signed a letter that a secretary brought to show him. And Leila remained there, waiting for him eventually to look at her and explain why she had been summoned. But Mister Knowlton didn't even bother to look at her. He continued every so often to put his finger between his eyelid and the glasses, which made Leila think this must just be one of his customary gestures.

She scrutinized him. He was blonde, an ashen blonde; his skin was dark, and his eyes blue or grey, it was impossible to tell from behind the lightly tinted glasses. He had a well-defined mouth, a hooked nose, a broad forehead divided almost geometrically into squares by two very prominent parallel wrinkles. He had thick dark blonde eyebrows, and his hair was combed back simply and in a manner that was far from attractive. Cropped short, it was thinning but made him appear virile.

A calm short voice removed Leila from her contemplation: "Miss Heimer."

A secretary hurriedly came towards them: "She's here, Mister Knowlton."

He looked from one side to another before eventually fixing his gaze on Leila. As Dolly had said, he had eyes like daggers. "Stand up," he proclaimed without emotion. Leila rose slowly. She stood firm in front of him, feeling neither fear nor weakness. She was a brave young woman, who knew what was right and what was wrong. That hateful beast wasn't going to intimidate her. "Are you Leila Heimer?"

"Yes, Sir."

"Are you related to Marie Heimer?"

"No."

"Good. I've got your file here. You worked for an advertising firm in New York." He fell silent, and placed his fingers under his glasses to remove them, leaving them on top of an envelope containing some papers on the huge table, and rubbed his eyes.

"I worked there until it went under."

He rolled his eyes up quickly. In a harsh voice he said, "here you only speak when you are spoken to."

"Sorry, Sir."

"You come highly recommended. I hope," he added bluntly, "that you won't let standards slip."

She didn't respond. He continued with the same tone of voice: "You can leave now." Leila turned around. With a cold gesture, Mister Knowlton removed the envelope containing the references for Leila Heimer as if the matter had now been forgotten. And, in fact, it had been. As she walked out, Leila heard: "Come in, Mister Bley." Leila heard the door closing slowly and walked down the corridor. She breathed deeply.

"What did you make of him?" asked Dolly on seeing her come in.

"How am I meant to know? It's not easy to get a handle on a guy like that."

"Of course not. Didn't I tell you? But, I wasn't exaggerating when I described him as a monster, was I?"

"Possibly not. The absolute," and she lowered her voice, "cretin had me waiting there for a quarter of an hour without even noticing me."

"He always does the same. But don't go thinking there's some kind of game plan behind it. It's just the way he is. Did you find him interesting?"

"He is."

"Yes," admitted Dolly reluctantly. "He's a cold fish, but girls like him. Anyone who makes enquiries about him in the dance-halls where the posh folk in Springfield spend their time will find that out."

CHAPTER III

The days went by, nearly two months elapsed, and life for Leila and her family had turned into a succession of calm and tranquil hours, with no unexpected surprises. Rob had nice handwriting, and assisted his sister in addressing those envelopes which ensured that he and Martha were able to continue their studies.

When Leila returned home that evening, Eve greeted her with an expression of fear on her face. "Leila, a young woman from your aunt's household has paid us a visit." Leila didn't want anyone interfering in her home. She had wiped the name of Miss Marie out of her life, and definitely didn't want her to pop up again.

"Why did she come?" she asked angrily.

"She said her mistress was expecting you today at eight o'clock."

"Expecting me?"

"Yes, you. I was also surprised, and I communicated that to her. She was very insistent."

"Alright. I'll go. What do you think they might want from me?"

"Maybe she's softened, and has had second thoughts."

"I don't want her to have second thoughts. I'm happy without her help. I adore my siblings, and she hates them. I'm not able to accept the favours of someone who detests my younger brother and sisters."

"Time takes its toll. Leila. Your aunt must have wound up very lonely."

"Lonely? No, Eve. Aunt Marie isn't made to live with anyone. Daddy always said she was unbearable."

"That's what being a spinster does for you …"

"She was very young back then."

"But hardly a beauty," said Eve ironically.

Leila smiled. "No, she's not exactly a beauty nor was she ever. She never forgave Mother for her looks or for being so down to earth, and the fact she then married twice."

"It's half past seven, Leila. If you're going to arrive for when she asked, you haven't got any time to waste."

"I'll make a move." She put a coat over her shoulders and, after blowing Eve a kiss, went out onto the street. She took the first omnibus she came across. It took her to a square next to the residential avenue over which her aunt's noble mansion towered haughtily at the edge of the district. There were many other mansions dotted along the avenue but the one belonging to the Heimers was the biggest. Leila shuddered on thinking that her father had once lived there. He had married the young and beautiful young woman that her mother had been at that time. James Heimer was a rich man, but his dabbles in the stock market had been disastrous. His capital reduced. Then Leila was born. Her father died when she was eight, leaving her mother responsible for everything. The money ran out. One day, she decided to re-marry. Her new husband was good to Leila, so good that she began to forget her real father, and blindly considered the man she lived with to be her Dad.

After pushing open the large gate, she walked slowly across the park. Leila preferred not to dwell on the past; it didn't do her any favours. First her step-father died, followed by her mother. It was all so painful. She rang the doorbell. A young maid let her in.

"I'm Miss Leila."

"Yes, yes, do come in. My mistress is expecting you."

Leila was overwhelmed by the luxury around her. She'd never want to live in a house like that. She could only remember a pretty flat, full of tenderness but then pain. They moved from that pretty flat to one that was less so, before winding up in a very humble abode.

"Leila, come in." She obeyed. As had been the case two months ago, Aunt Marie was sunken into the high-backed arm chair. By her feet, the dog the size of the pony slept on the thick carpet. "Come in and take a seat," invited the lady.

"I thought, Aunt Marie, you didn't want to be reminded that we were related."

"You're so impertinent. Come closer and take a seat."

"Will it take long to say your piece?"

"It will take as long as I see fit. And you can get rid of that irritating little tone of yours. I told you to take a seat."

She took a seat. The lady looked her up and down. She smoked through a long amber cigarette holder, exhaling the smoke slowly.

* * *

"I have to admit," as she brought her examination to a close, "that you are pretty."

"Am I meant to say thank you?"

"What you should do is listen, that's what you should do."

"I'm listening."

"I'm not lonely," clarified Aunt Marie without emotion, "but I don't have anything to keep me going through life. You could perform that role."

"Me?"

"Let me finish. I've decided that you ought to leave that stupid job and come and live with me. Don't move," she said, observing the young woman's movements. "I've not finished."

"You know my response."

"I know what you said when your mother was alive. She's not here anymore."

"Aunt Marie."

"Wait. Then you can tell me what you think."

"I can tell you now."

"I told you to wait."

"Alright …"

"I've decided you ought to live with me. I'll treat you superbly, you will live here as if you were my daughter. I'll give a party for my friends, introduce you into society and you'll be able to find yourself a good husband."

"Have you finished?"

"No."

"Well, carry on."

"Leila, you are just like your father. I can still remember his impertinence and pride. And what good did they do him?"

"They made him happy."

"So that he then had to bow to others. He who was so footloose and fancy-free. A man with prejudices befitting a man from his social class. And how did he end up? As a poor and wretched man."

"I've told you, he was happy. What does happiness mean to you?"

"Something you've yet to understand."

"You're wrong, Aunt Marie. I understand because it's something I experience. If I have more or less money, that doesn't bother me. Happiness can't be measured by a fistful of dollars."

"I didn't call you here to listen to you hold forth on a subject I believe you've yet to grasp. Let's just say that you are prone to sentimentality, and leave it at that."

"I'm proud of the fact. Why should I renounce it?"

"Do you have an answer for everything?"

"You talk, so do I. I don't think you've called me here to deny me that fundamental right."

"You're a foolish girl, there's no question about it."

"Have you finished yet, Aunt Marie?"

"No. I've been thinking of sending your siblings to school."

"Listen."

"A state school," she added, ignoring the interruption. "I'll give them a trade."

"You can stop right there."

"What's wrong with you?"

"I don't need your help. I can endure hunger, thirst and renounce even those things that seem most necessary, as long as I have the affection of my siblings. Is that clear, Aunt Marie?"

"Sit down, you stupid girl!"

"No, I've heard quite enough."

"Take care with how you respond, Leila. It'll be the last time I try to retain you."

"You're wasting your time."

"You're not trying to persuade me to look after those three bastards, are you? The children of a man I've never met?"

"Have I asked for your help?" asked Leila, pale with indignation.

The lady smiled sarcastically. "Of course not," she said scornfully. "I've no illusions over the fact you'd rather go hungry than call on me. And also that you'd rather call on anyone other than your aunt; but you carry my blood, you're a Heimer, and I have the duty to support you."

"I won't accept your charity, Aunt Marie. Neither will I thank you for it. You offended my mother before she became your sister-in-law. You offended her even more when she was left alone, without the solace of her husband, and you tried to take from her the only thing she had left, me. Then you offended my siblings. I may carry your blood, but I'm not proud of the fact."

"Leila!"

Boling over, Leila continued: "They really do carry my blood, and nothing in the world could make me abandon them. I also warn you that I wouldn't accept your help even if you offered to support the four of us."

"Get out …"

"And bear in mind that I won't set foot here again even if you call me. Goodbye, Aunt Marie."

The lady didn't respond.

* * *

Dolly and she crossed a plush street that Sunday afternoon. Passing in front of a dancehall, Dolly exclaimed: "I've always dreamt of being a pretty young girl, having a well-heeled boyfriend, and leaving a place like this on his arm. And, as you can see," she started to laugh uncontrollably, "I've not succeeded in finding either a well-heeled boyfriend or a husband."

"But, Dolly," said Leila, getting annoyed, "you always put yourself down and speak as if you're certain you're always going to be single."

"And what do you expect me to do? Burst into tears?"

"You're still young. You could still marry?"

"Yes, of course," Dolly mocked calmly. "I can get married whenever I want to the local butcher. He's professed his love to me for time immemorial. But if I was going to get married to a fat guy covered in grease and pork, smelling of cheap tobacco, I'd rather put up with the tyranny of Mister Ogre. Ah," she added in a low voice, "look who's coming out."

"Who?"

"The ogre. Look behind you, discretely." Leila did as she was instructed. The elegant society man emerged from the dance-hall, crossing the street and climbing into a ridiculously posh black car, which he had parked just off the square.

"He's on his own."

"He's always on his own."

"One day, he'll end up a catch for some rich heiress," laughed Leila.

"I guess so."

The car set off, and passed by them. The driver didn't even look at them. "He's a complete imbecile," grumbled Dolly. "He didn't even recognise us."

"And does that surprise you? He's over-worked, and his firm employs hundreds of people."

"But you're a head-turner."

Leila laughed good-naturedly. "And you reckon pretty girls interest Mister Ogre?"

"How am I meant to know? I think the only thing he's interested in is making life difficult for others." The car drove off into the distance, and the two friends kept walking, immersed in their childlike banter.

On arriving home, Eve rushed out to greet Leila. She seemed worried. "What's happened?"

"It's Rob."

Leila shuddered. "What's wrong with Rob?"

"I've been keeping an eye on him for days. He's pale and has a cough. This afternoon he came to me saying he was cold, and I took his temperature. He's running a high fever."

"What?"

"Yes. Go and see him. But don't let it scare you. It'll pass."

Leila ran to his room. Rob smiled at her from his bed. She kissed him tenderly. Leila loved all three of her siblings, but he had a special place in her heart for he was the one who gave her most support. He was almost a grown man, and had an adult mind. The fondness was mutual. "Rob."

"Eve is easily scared."

"Are you still feeling cold?"

"No, not any more. I'm going to get up. I'll help you address the envelopes."

"Don't even think about it."

"But, Leila."

"No, darling."

"It's all Eve's fault. She's so quick to jump to conclusions."

"Quiet, now. I'm going to call a doctor." The doctor came around straight away. He lived locally, and was known for being a good medic and a decent human being. After listening to Rob's chest carefully, he left the room without saying anything. Leila followed him out. The medical practitioner went into the bathroom to wash his hands. He was deep in thought. With a towel in her hand, Leila asked with concern: "Doctor, what is it?"

"Is he your brother?"

"Yes."

"You've not being taking all that good care of him."

"Doctor," she exclaimed with fear. "Has Rob got something serious?"

"Not necessarily serious, but something that needs to be taken care of. He's grown too quickly, and he's not strong. If he's not looked after, it could deteriorate into something serious. To be on the safe side, take him to a specialist first thing tomorrow. He'll provide the right treatment." Curiously looking about the place, he asked: "Are you insured?"

"No, Sir."

"Pity. In my opinion, this is a long-term illness."

She was overcome with fear. Her legs started to tremble and she had to hang on to the door frame to stop herself from falling. "But I can ask in the factory where I work," she suggested almost in a whisper.

The doctor's head twitched in an ambivalent gesture. "It would be best to visit a private specialist. My recommendation would be Dr Weld."

"Thanks Doctor."

CHAPTER IV

∿

A nurse helped Rob to get dressed in the adjacent room. In the consulting room, the studious and somewhat distant Dr Weld noted something down in a work book. In front of him was Leila, silent but trembling with trepidation.

"Miss Heimer," the doctor said suddenly, without taking his eyes off the work book, "I fear your brother will need to be hospitalized."

She was terrified. "Hospitalized," she repeated as if she were simple.

The specialist raised his cold and dark eyes. It was clear that he was accustomed to his patients' pain, which didn't affect him. He couldn't feel sorrow for all the family members of the patients who passed through his clinic on a daily basis. He raised his shoulders and said, "I'll be in a position to provide you with more details later this afternoon. Come back at seven o'clock and I'll have the results of the analysis and the radiography. I can, however, tell you now that your brother is at a very critical age and he's anaemic; it's dangerous and, if it gets worse, could even be life-threatening."

"Doctor."

"I'm sorry," he said without conviction. "Come back at seven."

She called for a car to take Rob home. Leila felt as if she was about to faint, although she made sure Rob didn't notice. She was no longer thinking about the studies that Rob would have to give up, but rather the optimistic lively lad she could suddenly envisage confined to bed in a sanatorium. It'd be horrible. As soon as they got home, she made Rob go to bed and locked herself in her room to cry. Eve tried to comfort her, but no words or logic could console the terrible pain Leila felt in her heart. And this pain, like a fire in her heart, was yet to know the terrible things that still awaited her. That her peaceful calm life was going to turn into unyielding desperation. But Leila didn't want to imagine that. She was crying for Rob. What did she matter? What else mattered apart from Rob's illness? She wasn't thinking about herself, or of Rob's studies that would be held up to an alarming degree, or in the money that the illness would cost, money she didn't have. Her only thoughts were for Rob. He was now a young man, with a keen sense of responsibility, and he'd suffer on both his own and her behalf.

"Leila …"

"Leave me be. Let me cry, Eve. I'm going to need to have my wits about me, to summon all of all my strength and courage to cope with the situation, but for now, leave me be to get things out of my system."

"You still don't know anything for definite," reassured the maid. "Doctors sometimes get things wrong."

"That specialist knew exactly what he was saying. Don't you realise Eve?" she wailed, raising her face bathed in tears. "Rob in a sanatorium."

"Calm down, my dear."

It was two in the afternoon on a beautiful spring day. The sun came through the window, bathing the room and shimmering off Leila's hair. On the surface, everything looked idyllic and, suddenly, Leila felt hateful towards everything, the sun, people crossing the road, her job …

"I forgot to tell you, Leila, your friend called round."

She sat upright suddenly in bed. "My god, I forgot about the office completely."

"Dolly was scared. She said that Mister Leigh had been asking after you. She added that you shouldn't stop going to work."

"Didn't you explain the situation to her," she said quietly.

"Of course, but she said the bosses won't take that into account. She said when you book an appointment with the doctor, that you should ask for a time outside office hours. She also said she'd explain the situation to Mister Leigh, but that you should make sure not to miss the afternoon shift. Have something to eat, darling, and I'll look after Rob until you get back."

"My God," Leila exclaimed, wiping her tears dry with a single swipe. "On top of this pain that's gnawing away at me inside, the nightmare of possibly losing my job."

"You won't lose it. Dolly said that both she and Mister Leigh will endeavour to conceal the fact you didn't turn up. And, please, Leila don't let Rob notice you're crying."

"Don't you worry about that. Rob comes before me and everyone. He won't notice a thing."

* * *

"You can't just not show up."

"But I've already explained the reason to you."

"Yes, yes. But, imagine that Mister Ogre decided to do a tour of the place, as he is prone to do from time to time. He'd fire you without thinking twice."

"He'd take pity."

Dolly became impatient. "I've already told you that here there's money, but no pity. Mister Leigh is a good man, and you got your foot in the door due to his recommendation. He may be a distinguished servant, but he's a servant none-the-less, and he might be putting his own job on the line by concealing your absence. And, so you know, he's got a big family and is as much a slave to the wage as you are. Besides," Dolly reasoned compassionately, "if, with Rob ill, you lose your job, you'll have to beg around Springfield, and don't be thinking there will be many to lend you a helping hand."

"You're scaring me now, Dolly."

"I'm opening your eyes to reality."

Mister Leigh called her into his office an hour later. Leila's heart was beating fast as she went in. The office manager was behind his desk with a worried look on his face. "Come in, Miss Heimer."

"I'm sorry about what happened, Mister Leigh."

"Yes, I already know about what's happened from Miss Dolly. Believe me, I've very sorry to hear it."

"Thank you."

"My advice to you is to keep medical appointments outside of working hours. It's in your own interests, especially with the lad being ill. You'll need to be earning in order for him to recover. Tell me, Miss Leila, what did the Doctor say?"

She explained the situation to him. Mister Leigh remained pensive. "We could arrange an insurance policy for you, but it wouldn't cover him as he's only a half-brother, which is an injustice like so many in this life ...", he said with sadness. "On the other hand, a charity ward is hardly advisable. My advice is that you send him to the Wilmes sanatorium. It's the best for such cases."

"But it'll cost money."

"Yes," he added pensively. "A lot of money. And the worst thing is you have to pay up front, or they won't admit him, and the rates aren't exactly low."

"I don't have a cent to my name."

"It's all such a shame," and he smiled, trying to cheer her up. "Maybe we're getting ahead of ourselves, Miss Leila."

"I'll know all the details at seven o'clock."

"Tell me what happens tomorrow."

She returned to her desk. She worked as if she were a robot. In the end, just before they clocked off, Dolly had to finish the work she was unable to get done. They left together. Leila held back the tears. Dolly was trying to reassure her. "I'll come with you," she offered. "Do you have money on you?"

"No. Why would I need it?"

"To pay for the diagnosis, my dear. Dr Weld doesn't do it out of the kindness of his heart. It's his work and he won't let a cent go astray."

"My god! We're at the end of the week. I don't have anything."

"I'll lend it to you," and, laughing effusively, "I'm hardly made of money, but I'll go without the cinema for the rest of the month."

"No, you can't give that up."

"Come on, don't be stupid." And, with that decided, she dragged Leila towards the doctor's house, which was very close by. He received them straight away, with the same cold indifference he had displayed in the morning. The results of the analysis and the radiography laid out on the table, he explained Rob's illness in a professional tone of voice. He needed to be hospitalised as soon as possible, and Dr Weld advised against a charity ward, which he said were hardly ever equipped to deal with long-term and contagious illnesses. His recommendation would be the Wilmes sanatorium. It might not be cheap, but it was the best if they wanted a happy ending. He went through everything with the monotonous voice of someone well accustomed to providing such explanations without being bothered by the final outcome.

Leila decided to have her say, and stated brusquely: "I don't have the necessary funds to pay for that sanatorium."

He looked at her with his eyebrows raised. He was an older man, of around fifty-six, with grey hair and an inexpressive face. "That's unfortunate," he said. And he stood up to indicate that the exchange had come to an end.

Dolly asked pleasantly, "And if we can show that Miss Heimer doesn't have the funds, that she's in fact quite destitute, having to work to support her three orphaned siblings."

"The management and specialists in the clinic do not take their clients' economic problems into consideration. If that wasn't the case, Miss," he added more softly, "they would have gone bankrupt a long time ago."

"But it's a sanatorium," added Dolly stubbornly. "A health centre, doctor."

"That doesn't mean that it isn't a business like any other for those who run it."

"But they can't just leave a patient to die."

"Of course not. There are hundreds of public hospitals."

"But not ones that you'd recommend," clarified Dolly bluntly.

"Quite right. An illness of this gravity requires attentive care and the right specialists. I'm sure there are some in paupers' hospitals, but none that I can recommend. I'm sorry."

Leila stood up. "How much do I owe you?"

"Fifty dollars."

The two young women were stopped still in their tracks. It was exactly the amount Dolly had on her. She deposited it on the table, picked up the radiography and the analysis, and said: "Leila, let's get out of here." They both left without saying goodbye. Dr Weld shrugged his shoulders indifferently.

* * *

"Okay, so what do I do now?"

"Stop crying for a start." Leila covered her mouth with a handkerchief and stifled a hoarse groan. "Leila," Dolly reproached vigorously, "if you give in to tears, we're not going to be able to think straight. What's needed is for you to stop thinking with your heart, and start being practical."

"Practical? You can't imagine how much I hate Dr Weld."

"He preys on those less fortunate than himself. Don't even mention his name to me." They were in Dolly's small apartment. Leila collapsed into a chair. Dolly was pacing from one side of the room to another. "We need to think. Neither of us have any money. Might it be worth asking for a loan at the factory?"

Leila got up, ready for action. "Yes, Dolly. First thing tomorrow I'll ask about it."

Dolly wasn't in the least enthused. "Wait Leila. Let me think."

"As far as the money's concerned, there's nothing to think about. The factory will offer me a loan."

"Listen, Leila, I don't want you to build your hopes up. The factory lends money to its employees to furnish their homes. It provides them with a flat and doesn't charge rent or bills, but I don't have the slightest idea about whether they'd lend any more money."

"But if I explain the situation."

"That's the only way. The best thing would be to ask Mister Leigh's advice tomorrow morning. He'll support you as much as he can. But bear in mind you're going to need a lot of money, and the factory might say no, thinking it excessive."

"I'll go without food. I'll return every last dollar they lend me."

"Yes, I know you will, but with that ogre."

"Him? Why would he need to get involved," shuddered Leila.

"If Mr Knowlton Sr. were alive, you wouldn't have to explain much, but his son is not like his father. The request will be sent above and it will be his decision. As I told you, Mister Ogre pokes his nose into everything."

"He'll take pity. If needs must, I'll go down onto my knees in front of him."

Dolly curved her lips into a sardonic smile. "It won't affect Mister so and so in the least that you're willing to bend down in front of him. If he wants to say no, he'll say no even if you're on your knees for three days in front of his lordship."

"My God … What should I do?"

"As soon as you get home, reassure Rob, and talk to him as if nothing has happened. Don't mention the sanatorium. Tell him that he'll just need to stay in his bed for a few days. Then you need to get some sleep, stop crying, and book an appointment to see Mister Leigh tomorrow. He'll be able to advise you."

"Dolly. If you weren't here."

"Come on," interrupted Dolly, hiding her emotion. "It's nothing really."

"I feel really lonely, Dolly."

"Well cheer yourself up. In situations like this, it's important to keep a clear head. And to be rational. Keep it in mind."

"The fifty dollars."

"Don't mention it. I hope Dr Weld chokes on them."

Leila hugged Dolly in silence. When the door closed behind her, Dolly crossed her arms, philosophically shaking her head on realising that she didn't have a cent with which to prepare dinner. "I'll go to bed on a empty stomach," she smiled calmly. "Dieting is no bad thing from time to time. To eat for the rest of the month, I'll ask Tim for credit. He'll give it to me. Him being in love with me has to serve for something."

CHAPTER V

~

Mister Leigh listened to Leila without blinking. When she had finished, he lit a cigarette and exhaled some smoke before responding. His voice was measured, almost unsettling. "It's a huge problem, Miss Leila. The amount you'll have to ask for is substantial. And I fear that management will view the request as excessive, perhaps even an abuse of your position."

"Mister Leigh," she lamented.

"Let me finish. First and foremost, I believe it's my obligation to inform you that were it anyone but you, I'd not allow this request to go forward. But taking into account the situation, and the fact it's you we're dealing with, I will make the request on your behalf although I ought to warn you that, in theory, we're prohibited from entertaining let alone encouraging petitions of this kind."

"I can't thank you enough, Mister Leigh."

The gentleman smiled tentatively, with a hint of bitterness. "I'm putting myself in your situation, Miss Heimer. I have eight children … I'll request a meeting with the head of personnel. You can return to your desk, and I'll call you in due course. But … don't go getting your hopes up. A few years ago … well that was very different."

An hour later, Mister Leigh announced in a somewhat timid voice over the intercom: "Come to my office, please, Miss Heimer." Leila stood up and headed over as if she were a robot.

"Leila," Dolly said softly, "don't get your hopes up. I don't think …"

"Please, let me believe that people as kind as you will cross my path." Dolly simply smiled, her stomach in knots about the dreadful situation facing that amazing young woman and those three humble motherless children.

Mister Leigh was standing next to the huge window. His worried look was enough to make the young woman shudder. "Mister Leigh."

He turned around to look at her. "Come in and close the door behind you, Miss Leila." The young woman did as instructed. "The news I have for you is … awful."

"Mister Leigh"

"It hurts me as much as it hurts you, believe me. And I have no doubt that it also pains the head of personnel. But there's nothing we can do. It's totally forbidden to request loans."

"But …"

"I'm sorry."

"Mister Leigh … I can't."

"I'm putting myself in your place. Would you like some advice?"

"Yes, oh yes."

"Ask for help from a paupers' hospital. We'll look for someone who can get your foot in the door, and trusted specialists will take care of your brother."

"No, not that."

"Miss Leila."

"I know that the sadness would kill Rob."

"Heavens above," exclaimed the kindly man. "Why don't you request a personal audience with Mister Knowlton? He's heartless," he added ominously, "but he might just soften on hearing of your situation."

"Do you think he will agree to see me?"

"Yes, I'm sure. He might laugh in your face, but he'll grant you an audience."

"I'll go then. I wouldn't ask anything for myself, but for Rob …"

"He hasn't come into the office this morning, but he'll definitely be in this afternoon. Don't mention either my name or the head of personnel. Go to see him, and explain the situation. Just that."

"Yes, I'll go. And thanks for everything, Mister Leigh."

"You know that if I had the money …"

"I know, I know. Thanks again."

She went before she burst into tears. She told Dolly what had happened. "I'll go and see Mister Knowlton."

"He won't see you."

"I can but try."

"I'd do the same in your situation but, as I've said before, don't go getting your hopes up."

* * *

Three women and a man, all secretaries to Mister Knowlton, were there in the office when she went in. Addressing a man, even if that man were Mister Knowlton, wouldn't be that difficult, but Leila was taken aback by the idea of others listening in. She decided to ask for a private meeting. And that's what she said to a young and elegant blonde (undoubtedly his personal secretary), who came towards her.

"How can we help, Miss Heimer?"

"I would like to speak to Mister Knowlton alone."

"In that case, you'll have to wait an hour. Return to your desk, and I'll personally phone you when he's ready to see you."

"Thanks. You're very kind."

The young woman looked at her attentively. "My name is Mirna Leigh."

"Oh."

"Be discreet," and looking to the end of office where, on the other side of the table, Mister Knowlton was to be found, added: "Within the hour, the four secretaries will have returned to their desks. That's when I'll request a meeting on your behalf. I hope Mister Knowlton doesn't refuse to see you."

It was a horrible hour of nervous tension. Dolly spoke to try and take Leila's mind off things, laughing about Mister Ogre's glasses, the rich heiresses who dreamt of having his hand, about herself, and the typewriter she ceaselessly bashed away on. The phone finally rang and Miss Leigh said, "You can come up now. Be quick."

"Thanks, Miss Leigh."

"Good luck", the personal secretary wished her succinctly.

Dolly stood up, and went towards Leila to give her a big silent hug. After holding her tight with her strong arms (I've not mentioned before that Dolly was tall, broad and fat, her body as big as her heart) and, looking her in the eyes, whispered: "Leila, don't cry. Remember that tears won't get you anywhere with that man. Explain what's happened briefly, with short clear phrases."

"I will do, but don't be getting your hopes up that I'll get anywhere with short clear phrases."

"I don't think, Leila, there are masculine or feminine techniques that will turn that man. Good luck!"

On exiting the elevator, Miss Leigh came out to greet her. "Miss Leila …"

"'I'm ever so grateful, Mirna."

"Bah. Don't mention it. Daddy rang me to warn me about your visit. Just so you are aware, Mister Knowlton isn't expecting you."

"Then …"

"Ask permission, go in and speak … If he had known you were coming, he would have asked the reason for your visit, and you would have had to explain to one of his secretaries."

"I'm ever so grateful."

"Be careful. And, above all, don't go into too many details. Mister Knowlton tires easily listening to things that don't concern him."

"I'm his employee, and I'm having to deal with a huge problem."

Mirna was moved, and smiled. "Yes, Leila, I know. But don't forget that someone who's never had to experience problems of this type is unlikely to be sympathetic to those who have. You have to experience something to understand what it means. And Mister Knowlton was a spoilt child, then a care-free teenager, and has no problems now as a grown man."

"Right."

"Good luck."

"Thanks."

* * *

Leila knocked on the door and opened it straight away. The man sat behind a board table covered in papers and maps didn't even look up. In his brusque cold voice, he said: "I've not summoned anyone." Leila didn't respond. Then Stephen Knowlton raised his eyes and removed his tinted glasses with a brusque gesture. "Who are you? What do you want?"

"My name is Leila Heimer."

"Fine, but what is it?"

"I want to speak with you, Sir."

"I've got three women and a man doing secretarial duties for me. They can listen to you. Go and speak to them."

"It has to be you."

"What?"

"I beg you to listen to me."

Stephen looked at her curiously. She was a pretty young thing, yes very good looking. "What are you doing in this office?" he asked, suddenly paying her attention.

"I am an employee."

"Ah," and losing interest, "if you have any complaints, write them down and send them to Mister Leigh." And putting his glasses back on, his eyes returned to his paperwork.

"I don't have any complaints."

He looked up quickly. "Haven't you worked out that I'm not willing to waste my time."

"Mister Knowlton …, I …"

Yes, she was a real looker. She had lovely eyes and an inviting mouth. How had he never noticed her? "You're new."

No, Mister Knowlton. I've been to this office before, on your request.

"Ah," he said, raising his shoulders. "I don't remember. Please, go back to your desk and say whatever you need to say to one my secretaries."

"I beg you to listen to me."

"Miss."

"Heimer."

"Fine, Miss Heimer, I've told you …"

"Sir, it's a very sensitive subject for me."

His Lordship's relaxed lips tensed up. "Well, spit it out and stop wasting my time."

"My brother is ill …"

"Take him to the doctor," he interrupted, going through his paperwork.

"I already have."

"This invoice hasn't been checked."

"Sir …"

"But are you still here?"

"I need to have him interned in a sanatorium."

"What?"

"I'm talking about my brother, Sir!"

Stephen stopped rummaging through his papers, put his fingers between the glasses frame and his eyes, and barked: "I couldn't care in the slightest what you do with your brother, Miss ... what did you say your name was again?"

"Heimer. Leila Heimer."

"The thing is my brother's dying," she said in a pained voice.

A pretty way of looking. Pretty hair. Everything about her was pretty. Although she obviously wasn't the sharpest pencil in the box. "When he dies, they'll give him a Christian funeral, Miss Heimer. In Springfield we're not accustomed to leaving people unburied."

Leila lost her composure somewhat. She shuddered and, overcome with indignation, exclaimed: "You're a monster, that's what you are." Nobody had ever called Stephen Knowlton anything like that to his face. He was left looking at the young woman with sympathy. That was the way Stephen was, but nobody had clicked yet, because it hadn't occurred to anyone to test his patience.

"Did you say monster?"

Leila swallowed hard. "Yes, that's what I said."

"Very interesting. What the hell do you want from me, young woman? I don't think you want me to join in your tears for your brother."

"No. I need money to take him to a sanatorium and I want to ask you for a loan."

"Ah!"

"That's what I want from you. Or, more accurately, from the company."

"I am the company."

"Well, from you."

"There are no loans! You've got charity wards. What's this obsession with appearing more than you are?"

"It's not about my vanity."

"I'm not interested in what it's about. There are no loans! This company limits itself to helping employees set up home. We facilitate that home, and the favours end there."

"But my brother's dying."

He replied pitilessly, stretching out in his swivel chair: "We'll take care of the funeral."

At this point, Leila really lost her patience, putting everything on the line: "You're a merciless excuse for a human being."

His sense of entitlement and power seemingly precluded any feelings of compassion towards his fellow man. "How dare you?"

"That's just the beginning. I detest you. I detest you with every bone in my body."

On being left alone, Stephen wondered why he hadn't thrown the young woman out of the window. It was genuinely curious! As was the fact he wasn't really annoyed by her! Money? Yikes … An impassioned young woman who'd told him she despised him. A very pretty young girl, and besides … It gave food for thought. Why not give her the money? Yes, why not? He took a small pad out of his pocket, and noted down, "Leila Heimer." He'd bear it in mind, and the pretty face of the young girl that was … overflowing with emotion.

"Very passionate, indeed," he said to himself. "And very daring."

CHAPTER VI

~

"Now everyone knows all my business," finished Leila, letting herself fall into the depths of the chair as if she'd completely given up. Dolly and Mister Leigh looked at each other, both concerned.

"We did warn you, Leila. You've got to try and keep it together."

"My friend, you should have borne in mind that Mister Knowlton is up there and you are down here."

"His merciless words about my darling Rob were just too much for me, Mister Leigh."

"Yes, yes," he admitted. "I understand where you're coming from, but I can't forgive your attitude. You were warned, not just by me but also by Miss Dolly and my own daughter who, as you well know, arranged the meeting for you. That meeting, if approached with caution, could have been very productive. It's not any old employee who gets to see Mr Knowlton one-on-one."

"I'm sorry," she sighed, beside herself, covering her face with her hands. "I'm sorry for you, for your daughter, for me … Above all, I'm sorry for Rob," she said, drowning in tears and adding regretfully: "One can't always suppress legitimate pride. And Mr Knowlton set out to make me suffer from the word go. I lost it … It was only going to have one outcome." She stood up and moved towards the table. "I don't know what I'll do, but I'm sure not going to let Rob be interned in a charity ward."

She started to gather some of her personal possessions from off the table, concealing them in the depths of her leather handbag. "What are you doing?" asked Mister Leigh.

"Gathering my things together. I'll go to accounts and ask to be paid what I'm owed. I'd rather resign myself than be fired by him."

"No, Leila. As long as management doesn't send orders, you stay where you are."

"When the order comes from above, I'd rather be far away from here. I'll have to start looking for a new job. It's not going to be easy," she added bitterly, "but it's my duty." It was with sadness that she said, "I'm sorry for all the trouble I've caused you."

"Leila," intercepted Dolly, "don't leave unless they fire you."

"No, Dolly …"

"Yes, my dear. Put your pride to one side and think of Rob."

"That's right, think of Rob, Leila," Mister Leigh added quickly. "Because of him, you have the duty to put up with a lot of things. And, anyway, if they do try to fire you, let me try and apologise on your behalf."

"No, that I won't allow," she cried, unable to conceal her pain. "Under no circumstances will I let you put your job on the line."

"My duty is to defend my staff. You work under my command. I'll apologise, and you'll do as I do. For once in his life, Mister Knowlton will reveal a humanitarian side," he said, unconvinced.

Leila was going to respond when the curt, gruff and authoritarian voice of Mister Knowlton came over the intercom: "Mister Leigh to my office." The interference when the intercom was switched off made them collectively shudder as they looked at each other in turn.

"Mister Leigh."

"Calm down, Leila. It won't be long until we know what we're dealing with."

He headed to the door. Leila followed him, and touched him on the arm: "Mister Leigh. You know you've been called to the boss's office to be reprimanded for my daring. Don't apologise on my behalf Mister Leigh. I'm extremely grateful, but it's just not worth it. I'm going to be fired anyway, as I've said to him things that I doubt anyone's ever had the gall to say to his face." The office manager looked at her tenderly. He left without saying a word, fully convinced that Leila would be fired straight away.

After he had closed the door behind him, Dolly moved towards her workmate and placed a hand on her shoulder. "Leila," she whispered. "What's done, is done but ..."

"Yes, yes. I know I should have shown some restraint. But, there are things. My God! What's going to happen now to me and the little ones."

"I'll help you look for another job."

"You ... you also think ... that they'll fire me." Dolly carried on looking at her, without committing herself. "Dolly. Do you think?" Dolly nodded. They stood against the wall, staring at each other, until the door opened a few minutes later.

* * *

Mister Leigh smiled at them, radiantly.

"Mister Leigh," exclaimed Dolly. "What's happened?"

"Nothing, my dears. Absolutely nothing."

"But."

And Leila trembled. The gentleman moved towards her, touched her on the shoulder and said affectionately, "Get back to work, Leila. And don't give what's happened a second thought."

"Did he accept your apologies?", she asked, taken aback, in a quiet voice.

"No, not at all. I didn't need to apologise. He called me to his office about a completely different matter. He didn't mention you at all, and neither did I."

"Incredible," whispered Dolly.

"Yes, it is."

"He'll still have me fired."

"No, he won't. Leila. In situations like this, the order would have to come through me. And I can tell you that Mister Knowlton acts straight away in such cases."

"Then."

"You won't be asked to leave."

"But."

"I have to admit it's the first time the boss hasn't reacted to an employee's insolence." He laughed, and added, "Because you were insolent, Leila, even if you don't want to admit it."

"I admit it," conceded the young woman, breathlessly.

"And Rob …?"

"You'll need to request a bed in a charity ward?"

"No!"

"Leila, my dear girl …"

"No, Dolly. I'll do … anything. I won't allow Rob to die."

"Miss Leila."

"No, Mister Leigh. I'll speak to whoever, but I won't let Rob be forgotten in one of those hospitals where they count patients by the dozen."

* * *

That day, on arriving home, she sat at Rob's bedside. She caressed one of his hands with hers.

"Leila, how long am I going to be stuck in bed?"

"Well … no; you'll get better soon, just wait and see."

"Eve said they might have to take me to a sanatorium."

"Maybe, but I'd come and see you each and every day."

"Would they … let you?"

"Yes, don't you worry."

"Leila," said Rob in a pained manner, barely holding back the tears, "I don't want to go to a hospital like that one."

All of the siblings were traumatised by paupers' hospitals. That was where their mother had died. They would never forget it. That's why Leila would turn Springfield upside down before allowing Rob to go to one of those places. "If you leave this flat, Rob," she said effusively, "it will be to go to a private sanatorium, somewhere where I can remain at your side when I'm not working, where I can even sleep next to you."

"That sounds good, Leila."

"Yes, my darling, yes." And Leila ran off to cry desperately in her own room.

That evening, when Dolly and she left work, they walked silently in pensive mode. Dolly asked out of the blue: "Have you sorted anything out?"

"Nothing."

"Leila," she said hesitantly. "I think with the right contact, that he'd be well treated in a charity ward."

"No!"

"Why are you so appalled by the idea?"

Leila nestled her hands into her skirt pockets and, struggling to articulate her words, said: "That's where my mother died."

"Leila."

In a voice that didn't seem to belong to her, Leila added: "We were only allowed to go and see her once or twice a week … they told us she had died. They didn't even let us see her." She bit her lips as if she were holding back the desire to scream, and whispered: "That's why, Dolly, I'll do anything to prevent Rob from ending up in a place like that. Rob's got the same illness that killed my Mum. Back then, I was too young to understand. Now … it's different."

* * *

On entering the office the following morning, there was an envelope on her work-desk. Dolly saw it first and, on picking it up, shook it. "Leila, it's for you."

"The dismissal."

"No. Dismissals tend to be less formal."

"You open it. I don't dare."

"I'll do it." Dolly opened the seal straight away. "Incredible. Mister Ogre has booked you an appointment to see him in his office at eleven o'clock this morning."

"To fire me."

"No."

"Then, what can he want from me?"

"I don't know. It just says to wait for him in his office at eleven o'clock. And it's signed by his secretary."

"I'm trembling, Dolly."

"Well, cheer up. Get to work, forget about everything and, come eleven o'clock, freshen yourself up and off you go."

"What can he want from me?"

"You never know, there's a first for everything. Maybe he's decided to become a philanthropist, and will give you the money."

"Do you think?"

"No," she said firmly. "I don't think. I don't think Mister Ogre is capable of a good deed. But he'll have something to say."

"If you were me, what would you do Dolly?"

"Keep working and, at eleven o'clock, gather your thoughts and go … without losing control. I've never met anyone as unpleasant as Mister Ogre. It wouldn't surprise me if he's summoned you just to have a go at you."

"I won't be able to control myself. He'll get his answer."

"Not the best way of going about things. If he's decided to play games, that's just what he'll be looking for. He'll want you to lose it."

They returned to their work. At eleven, Leila made the sign of the cross, looked up to the ceiling and kissed the pendant that hung round her neck. "Give me strength," she whispered. "See you later, my darling. Pray for me."

Dolly looked at her tenderly. "I will do. And remember you have an obligation, and that you carry an image of the Virgin in whom you can trust around your neck."

"Yes, here's hoping that she remains at my side."

On crossing the corridor, she bumped into Mister Leigh who was coming out of his office. "Good day, Miss Leila. How is Rob?"

"The same."

"And ... you?"

"We'll see." She seemed out of it.

"With your permission, one of these days I'll take the liberty of paying your brother a visit."

"I'd be very grateful for it."

"You haven't given any more thought to the idea of a charity ward?"

"No!"

"If it were me ..."

"Yes, but ... I won't."

"Leila."

"No, Mister Leigh."

"But ... Why such hatred towards such places when the vast majority of them are excellent?"

"My mother ... died in one of them."

"Ah ...!", and then he said energetically: "But things don't always turn out that way."

"I'll never be able to forget the misery I went through, nor the sleepless nights thinking of a woman alone amongst strangers in a depressing common ward."

"I'll try to find someone on the inside, someone who can authorise you to sleep next to your brother."

"No. I'm very grateful, but no. I have to find something better."

"But, in the meantime, Rob won't get any better, and his condition might even deteriorate."

"I'll find a solution over the next three days."

And Leila suddenly thought about her aunt: Why not, after all? Aunt Marie was one of the richest women in Springfield, and she must deep down have a heart, for she was a human being after all. She'd promise to go and live with her, even if she'd rather flee to the end of the world with her three siblings than do so. But, by that time, Rob would be better.

"Miss Leila … What are you thinking about?"

"Ah! I'd forgotten you were there."

"Where are you going now, Leila?"

"Mister Knowlton has called me to his office."

"What?"

"Yes, and I'm heading there. See you later, Mister Leigh."

"Have you thought about what Mister Knowlton might want from you?"

"No."

"Take care with what you say, Leila. The boss has a forceful personality, and very little patience."

"I'll keep it in mind. Although it's difficult keeping my nerves in check."

"They need to be."

"Yes. Thanks for everything, Mister Leigh. Go and see Rob whenever you please. Wish me luck and patience."

"With all my heart."

Leila headed for the elevator, and Mister Leigh remained still, looking at her tenderly. He was fond of her. He could also imagine one of his kids in her place.

CHAPTER VII

~

Leila waited rigidly at the door. Stephen Knowlton looked up idly and curved his provocative mouth into a sarcastic smile. "Come in and close the door behind you, princess." Leila shuddered. Dolly was right. He had summoned her to make her suffer. To take pleasure in her suffering again and again. No doubt that was the reason he hadn't yet fired her. She would amuse him in his breaks from work. However, she closed the door and moved towards him. She didn't expect to be asked to take a seat. The two times he'd granted her an audience, she'd been kept standing as if he were a king and she a humble servant. That's why she was so surprised on hearing him say: "Take a seat, princess."

She didn't sit down. He rolled up his eyes, not hidden by glasses this time. They were grey and steely, as cold as knife blades. "I told you to take a seat." And he twitched the hands that held his glasses.

"I've abandoned my desk," she pointed out in that rebellious fashion of hers. "I'll need to get back as soon as possible."

"I'm in charge of your desk, princess," Stephen laughed in a way that made Leila shudder from her head to her toes, "and I'm ordering you to take a seat."

She forgot Dolly's and Mister Leigh's words of advice. Someone else in her place would have shown themselves to be docile and submissive. Not her. She had her pride and that man drove her mad. "You have received me here on other occasions and you kept me on my feet. I'm not tired. You can say whatever you have to say."

"Ha, ha," he exclaimed looking right at her. And in an odd tone of voice, he added, "you've got more character than I thought. Do you know something, Leila Heimer? I like you."

"How? What?"

"I like you," and, with irony, as he sprawled across the sofa and fidgeted with the glasses he still held in his hands, "I like you a lot. Don't take a seat if you don't want to, but listen to me." He leaned forward, resting his elbows on the table, holding his chin in his open palms. His glasses had now been abandoned to a corner of the desk. "Yesterday, you told me that you needed money."

"I still need it."

"How much?"

"A lot. It's for my brother's medical treatment, so he recovers."

He moved backwards and leaned his head a bit to the side. Without emotion, he said, "As you already know, I'm not in the least interested in the state of your brother's health. My only interest is in you," and with an indifference that shook Leila as if she had been hit by a hurricane: "I have become accustomed to reserving Thursdays for my indulgences. I'm going to invite you to spend those Thursdays with me in my mountain lodge. You'll have a car waiting for you wherever you like. That car will take you to the plot of land I own on the mountain, and will bring you back at the hour I see fit. The day after, you won't acknowledge me and I won't acknowledge you. In exchange," he added frostily, "you can take your brother to whatever sanatorium your heart desires. Now you know why I've called you up. You can leave now but provide me with an answer before next Thursday."

Such was the suffocation she felt that she gulped twice before mustering a response. All of her pride, anger and ferocity came out in these few words: "You're infinitely more of a swine that I had ever imagined. Good day, Sir."

"I warn you that I'm not usually so indulgent with my employees."

"Fire me."

"No. I hope you come to your senses," and, with a cynical smile, "you're beautiful and proud. That's what attracts me to you. I'll expect your answer before next Thursday."

"Never!"

"Never say never. We humans should avoid it all costs. Good day."

* * *

She left, with the desire to shout and scream. But she didn't. Once inside the elevator, she gritted her teeth, clenched her fists, and searched for some corner of her being in which to find the strength she was so sorely lacking.

"What did he want from you?" Dolly was in front of her. Leila needed to pretend. Nobody would ever know to what extent she'd been humiliated. No, nobody would ever find out. "What did he want? You look out of it."

"Nothing, he didn't want anything important … He reprimanded me for yesterday." "Did he? His Lordship was sufficiently wounded by your words, your insults affected him?"

"It looks like it."

"How odd!"

"Look at how behind I've got with my work!" And she went towards her typewriter. At that moment, Mister Leigh came in.

"Ah," he exclaimed on seeing her. "I didn't think you were back yet. What did Mister Knowlton want from you?".

"Nothing, he didn't want anything important … He reprimanded me for yesterday."

"Ah!"

"Doesn't it seem strange to you, Mister Leigh?" Dolly asked.

"Yes, very strange. It's the first time Mister Knowlton has ever reprimanded an employee. His rule is to fire them without warning," he smiled pacifically. "Better this way. You must be happy, Leila?"

"Yes ... very." And she wanted to scream. To scream in desperation until her parents heard her, until she lost her voice. Even until it killed her. Because Leila Heimer would rather die than dishonour the purity of her Thursdays ...

"You can now discount the possibility of being fired, Leila," said a satisfied Mister Leigh. "I'm happy for you Leila, I really am ..."

"Thank you ... Thanks, Sir."

And, that evening, on leaving the office and bidding farewell to Dolly, she decided to visit her aunt. It was her last resort for finding a remedy for Rob's health. She would cry, she would be humiliated, she would go down on her knees ... Anything to get the money she needed for her brother to be cured. Anything ... apart, that is, from accepting that monster's awful proposition. The young maid who opened the door recognised her. She smiled and said she'd tell her mistress that she was here. Almost instantly, the maid returned. "Follow me, Miss Leila." She followed in silence. And as she saw her aunt covered by a blanket, sunken into the sofa with her feet next to the fireplace, and the dog lying down at her feet, Leila moved towards her.

"Hello ... Have you heard?"

"Heard what?"

"About my illness."

Ah, that's why the fire was on full in May. "I hadn't heard," she said sincerely.

"Right. Sit in front of me." And, sarcastically, once the young woman had taken her seat, she said: "If you'd have known I was ill, you wouldn't have come. Am I wrong?"

"I might have come earlier."

"Your good heart moves me."

"I've not come to listen to your set-pieces, Aunt Marie. You're right, I do have a good heart, or at least I feel my fellow-man's pain as if it were my own. I'm sorry you're ill."

"Why have you come?" she asked, cutting her short.

"Before that, I'd like to know what illness you're suffering from."

"If only I knew," she replied without emotion. "The doctors don't know either. They rehearse all their experiments on me, but they haven't reached any grand conclusions." And, scornfully, she added: "They're a bunch of donkeys. Why have you come?"

* * *

"I've asked you why you've come, Leila?"

"Do you suffer a lot, Aunt Marie?" she asked in an odd way.

The lady raised an eyebrow. "Where the hell does that question come from? You're not worried if I suffer or not. You want to take pleasure in my pain."

"I've never taken pleasure in anyone's pain," Leila replied with dignity. "Much less in yours."

"Very kind of you. But I asked why you've come."

"Aunt Marie," she begun softly, "I asked if you suffered because one who knows suffering is better placed to judge another who suffers."

"Ah, do you have angina or something?"

"Now's not the time for irony, Aunt Marie."

"If I want to be ironic, I will be."

"I'm referring to Rob."

The lady became impatient, and without the slightest hint of pity, exclaimed: "What do you want to tell me about that bastard?"

"Aunt Marie."

"That bastard," she shouted, beginning to lose her composure.

"Remember, Aunt Marie, you're ill and you shouldn't get worked up."

"Well don't speak to me of those three hateful lepers then."

"They are my blood, as I am yours."

"Them carrying my blood? That's quite enough, Leila. You carry my blood, but them …"

"Aunt Marie."

"Spit it out, won't you?"

"Yes. I think that would be for the best. I'm here to ask for your help."

"Help? The proudest girl alive comes down from her pedestal to ask a favour of her hateful relative."

"I've never hated you, Aunt Marie," Leila said sincerely. "Indifference, perhaps. Hatred, no."

"Tell me once and for all what this is all about." She put her hand on her chest and winced: "These palpitations …"

"Aunt Marie."

"Spit it out, Leila," she screamed, "and don't pity me."

"I need money."

"Ah," she laughed, stifling the pain that gnawed away at her. "Money? What do you want to buy? A car?"

"No, it's not for such whims," she replied bitterly. "It's for Rob. He's suffering from a delicate illness. From the same illness Mum died of for want of care."

"Ah, yes."

"Aunt Marie," she got it together to say: "Put yourself in my place. Rob needs to be interned in a sanatorium. As you know, that costs money."

"There are charity wards."

"Mum died in one of those."

"You'd have more peace and quiet if Rob were also dead."

"Aunt Marie!"

"I won't take any of it back."

"Aunt Marie, if you weren't ill, I'd give you the answer you deserve."

"Go right ahead. I'm not going to faint."

"Oh, Aunty. How cruel you can be about some poor defenceless children," and, in a persuasive tone of voice: "I promise that, once Rob recovers, I'll come and live with you … I promise, Aunt Marie! But … give me that money, or instruct the trustees of your estate to pay the sanatorium."

"No!"

"Aunt Marie!"

"I've said no. I won't give your siblings a cent. For you … whatever you want. But I won't give them anything."

"You are suffering, Aunty, you know what that means. You've lived. You've had everything. Rob is a child, we don't know what fate has in store for him. You, Aunt Marie," she added, unable to hold back the tears. The lady listened to her impassively. "You could save a human being from great suffering. Imagine if someone could alleviate yours."

"It's all useless, Leila," she exclaimed cruelly. "You're wasting your time."

Leila stood up. She could no longer control her sobbing. Petitioning her aunt had been her last resort, and she genuinely thought she would lend a helping hand. The fact that her options were running out tortured Leila. And she thought of Mister Knowlton and his black Thursdays … Her Thursdays that had always been innocent … and how they would be perverted! If they were perverted, it was only because she couldn't leave Rob to die.

"I'm tired of your crying, Leila. Go away."

"Aunt Marie," she said in a way that made the lady tremble, but did nothing to soften her resolve, "you are ill, you might die, and then you'll be held to account for your sins."

"Do me a favour, and keep your mouth shut."

"You'll be held to account for them, Aunt Marie," she continued unplacated. "Whatever happens to me from now onwards, on your conscience be it."

"You're a stupid little drama queen, Leila. You're turning something quite simple into a melodrama. And, on top of that, you're fatalistic. I pity you. If you had to earn your living as an actress, your performances would be pitiful and the audience would soon tire of you." Leila, without responding, turned around and left with her head held high. Aunt Marie smiled indifferently.

* * *

Rob fainted that night, and his temperature rose to an alarming degree. Leila, scared, called the medical practitioner, and he greeted Leila as follows: "How have you not yet sorted anything out for this poor lad? Dr Weld informed me that he should be interned without delay," and, determinedly: "If you don't do it within twenty-four hours, I'll have no option but to report you to the health centre."

"Doctor ..."

"Well just so you know, Miss Leila."

He headed to the patient's room and examined him carefully. He gathered his stuff together, and came out followed by a nervous and pale Leila. "Every hour spent in this house takes a day off your brother's life," insisted the Doctor, mercilessly. "Swear to me you'll seek help at the hospital; if not, I'll have to report you to the health authorities."

"I give you my word."

"Fine," he signed a prescription. "Do you know how to administer injections?"

"Yes, Sir."

"Take this to the nearest pharmacy; you can inject what they give you to put him to sleep."

"Is he is in such a bad way?"

The doctor looked at her calmly but, on seeing her troubled feminine expression, took pity and said softly: "Miss Leila, as long as they are treated promptly, these kinds of illnesses in a child aren't at all serious. Ignoring them doesn't do any good at all. If you put a sock on and you don't repair the holes straight away, they get worse and you have to throw the sock away. If you sew it up straight away, the sock will last for months and even years. And you might even throw the sock away for being old without the hole getting any bigger. Do you follow?"

"Yes ... yes, Sir."

"Well, this is what's happening with your brother. Nowadays these illnesses can be treated, as long as they are caught in time."

"But in a charity ward ..."

"Why not?"

"My mother died in one."

"A button falling off a jacket doesn't mean they're all going to fall off."

"But ..."

"A paid room in a good sanatorium would be better, but that's not within everyone's means, Miss Leila."

"I'll go private," she said without wavering.

The doctor looked at her with a certain admiration. But he limited himself to saying: "Better for you, and better for him. Good night, Miss Leila."

She went out, crossed the street and went into the pharmacy to ask for the drugs to inject. An hour later, Rob was asleep, almost still. Leila remained at his side until it was time for her to go to the office. Her mind was blank. She could think only of Rob, of her dead mother, in the horror the idea of a general ward inspired in her. What did she matter? She would immunise herself from feeling.

Her thoughts would be restricted to practical as opposed to spiritual matters. And one day she'd find herself free of that sin. When the children were grown up and could fend for themselves, that would be the time for her to dedicate herself to the Lord. He, who knew her innermost being, would forgive and take pity on her. No, her spirit would never sin. And Rob's life depended on her ... Yes, only on her, on the decision she had to take. And ... it was already taken.

* * *

She didn't tell Dolly what had happened that night with Rob. She needed to make sure nobody suspected what she was going to do. She was restless first thing in the morning but, as the day progressed, her energy levels and spiritual reserves increased. It was almost as if she had been possessed by a mysterious power.

"Where are you going?" Dolly asked, intrigued.

"I'm going to Mister Knowlton's office."

Dolly opened her eyes widely. "What? Has he summoned you?"

"He made me an offer, yesterday."

"Ah." And Dolly was left with her mouth open. "What kind of offer?"

"I didn't tell you about it, because I had to think about my reply," she said, searching her mind for a plausible explanation. "I've now had the chance to think about it."

"You're confusing me, Leila. And I have to say you seem different."

"Well ... I'm the same as always."

"Explain yourself, then."

"As you know, Mister Knowlton isn't the kind of man who does favours out of the goodness of his heart. But he didn't disregard the possibility of helping me with Rob, if I accepted his proposition."

"And what proposition was that?"

"That I look after a blind relative of his in the mountains on Thursday."

"Ah. That's no bad thing. You'll accept, won't you?"

Leila closed her eyes forcefully, and opened them straight away. "Yes, I'm going to accept. The thing is it'll mean I can't go and visit Rob in the sanatorium on those days. But ... you'll go in my place, won't you?"

Dolly was an innocent abroad, so sincere and pure, that she thought her fellow-man incapable of lying. It was the first time Leila had lied and she asked God's forgiveness time and again in Rob's name. She ... no longer mattered at all ... She was Rob's health, and nothing else. When Rob recovered and was grown into a man, she could only hope he would be man enough to look after and care for his two younger siblings if the Lord took her away.

"Of course, I'll take care of Rob on Thursdays, Leila," Dolly enthusiastically exclaimed. "Accept, my dear. Looking after a patient must be easy for someone as accustomed to it as you. Is it just on Thursdays?"

"Yes," she replied in a low voice. "Just Thursdays. My ... Thursdays." And she left. Without pausing, she took the elevator. When it stopped on the floor for central administration, she walked out and stood stiffly in the corridor. Her legs were trembling. She thought of Rob, of her Aunt Marie, of her deceased parents. She looked up at the ceiling, gripped her heart with both hands, and whispered: "God forgive me. You know what I'm doing, and why." A superior force pushed her forwards. She wasn't aware of when she lifted her hand or who let it knock on the oak door.

"Come in," said a feminine voice.

She went in. As on other occasions, the three secretaries were working alongside Mister Knowlton and he, wearing his glasses, ignored her. All his attention was fixed on some paperwork he was reading through. "What can I do for you, Miss Leila?" Mirna Leigh asked, coming out to greet her.

"I need to speak to Mister Knowlton."

"He's ... busy. He can't see you at the moment."

"He told me to come here."

"Ah," and lowering her voice significantly. "Has something been sorted?"

"I think so ..."

"The boss?"

"Yes."

"Incredible. Wait here a moment."

She crossed the long and wide office, and said something to Mister Knowlton. He looked up idly, and gave a command that Leila couldn't hear, but that his lackeys didn't need to hear twice. The three of them, one after another, left and Mister Knowlton quickly said: "Come closer." Leila moved towards him. "Take a seat."

"I'm not tired."

"Take a seat I said," Stephen commanded brusquely as if he were about to lose his patience. A rebellious Leila ignored him and he smiled tepidly. "Breaking your pride is going to be no easy task."

"I accept your offer to care for your infirm relative on Thursdays."

"Oh," he laughed, getting over his surprise. "You've got your wits about you."

"I accept," and brusquely: "My brother needs to be interned into Springfield's best sanatorium, today."

"Agreed. I'll arrange for an ambulance to pick him up."

"Thursdays, and Thursdays only."

"Yes."

"As soon as Rob recovers, you won't see me again."

"I'll have tired of you before then ..." he laughed shamelessly.

"Nobody will know ... anything."

"Why not?" he laughed again, mockingly. "It's entirely reasonable for you to look after my poor relative on Thursdays in exchange for your brother's health."

"Fine," she uttered without emotion. Stephen Knowlton liked that feminine energy more and more. "It's an acceptable version."

"My car will wait for you on Thursdays in Venice Square. It's an isolated area, discrete. Do you know how to drive?"

"Yes."

"Ah. You do, do you," he laughed sarcastically.

"We had two cars when my parents were alive."

"Too many not to have even one now."

"I forbid you from meddling in my private life."

"Okay. I accept the prohibition. So that you know," he added dryly, "apart from on Thursdays, I won't have the slightest interest in you or your life. You can leave now."

Leila did an about turn. On returning to her desk, Dolly and Mister Leigh looked at her curiously. "You're so pale, Leila," Dolly exclaimed.

Leila wiped her forehead. "Mister Leigh," she said quietly. I won't be able to come to work this afternoon. I need to take Rob to a sanatorium."

"You've got what you set out to achieve," he said, without even needing to ask.

"Yes."

"Thank the Lord you've managed to soften Mister Knowlton's heart. Dolly has already told me everything."

She was going to respond when the dry brusque voice of Mister Knowlton came over the intercom: "Mister Leigh."

"Yes, Sir."

"Permit Miss Leila to clock off early. Within the hour, an ambulance will pick her brother up to take him to a sanatorium in Santa Barbara. And keep in mind that on Thursdays she will be looking after my Uncle Edward in the mountains. A car is to be made available for Miss Leila. This car will be in Venice Square on Thursdays to pick her up in front of the Health building."

"Anything else, Sir?"

"That's all."

And there was the cold sound of interference as the intercom was switched off. Leila, like a robot, stood up. Dolly exclaimed, full of joy, "Thank the Lord that everything is resolved. Laugh and be happy, Leila."

Leila mustered a tepid smile. A smile that was like a silent sob.

"Miss Leila," the gentleman said. "You don't know how happy I am that everything's been resolved." And, looking at Dolly, "We have to concede, Miss Dolly, that our boss isn't as inhuman as we had thought."

"Which I'm pleased about, Mister Leigh. I have to admit he's more honourable than I'd given him credit for."

"See you tomorrow," interrupted Leila, heading for the door.

"Miss Leila," the gentleman exclaimed," you have reasons to be cheerful, but you seem to be sad."

"It's hardly a laughing matter, Mister Leigh."

"Of course not. But you're going to leave your brother's health in good hands. So that you are aware, Mister Knowlton is one of the most influential men in the country. The Santa Barbara sanatorium is the best there is."

"Yes, right, I knew that already." She left slowly.

When the door closed behind her, Dolly and the gentleman looked at each other. "It looks as if she's carrying the weight of the world on her shoulders."

"It's hardly surprising, Mister Leigh. Bear in mind she's not going to be able to see her brother on Thursdays."

"Yes," admitted Mister Leigh calmly, "for a sister as caring and affectionate as Miss Leila, that's a horrible setback. But nobody gets what they want without making sacrifices."

CHAPTER VIII

～

On that afternoon (three days after Rob was admitted to the Santa Barbara sanatorium), Leila was heading down the street towards the bus, on her way to see him in the enclave on the outskirts of town, when an elegant make of car sidled up next to her. She was very familiar with that model of aerodynamic cars that had recently been launched by the Knowlton factory. They were very powerful cars, but the best belonged to Mister Knowlton. And he, seated in front of the wheel, looked at her strangely that afternoon.

"If you're waiting for the bus," he said, sticking his head out the window, "get in next to me. I'm heading in the same direction as the sanatorium." Leila didn't go red, but her body felt as if it were on fire, like a tremor that shook her intensely. The next day was Thursday ... Uncle Edward's Thursdays. She was about to get in next to him, to beg him for some mercy, to cry, to humiliate herself ... but, on meeting his eyes, she realised Stephen Knowlton wouldn't take pity on her or anyone. "Climb in, Miss Leila."

"Thanks, but I'd rather go by bus."

He laughed calmly. "You aren't," he said sarcastically, "very diplomatic."

"I don't pretend to be."

"Do us both a favour, climb in."

"I'd rather stay here, and catch the bus."

In lieu of a response, he opened the car door and abruptly commanded: "For your own good, get in and don't make me insist. You'll make a scene, and that'll be worse."

She would get in, and say to him ... Yes, she'd tell him to show mercy on her, on her status as a woman, her purity. She climbed in, and the car driven by Stephen Knowlton sped off. There was a silence she interrupted with a quiet voice: "Mister Knowlton ..."

"Yes."

He didn't look at her. His disconcertingly steely eyes were looking straight ahead. "I, Mister Knowlton ... I assure you ...", she shuddered. She pressed her fingers against her mouth.

"Well, don't stop there," he coldly ordered. "What is it that you want to assure me?"

"I am very grateful for what you've done for Rob," she said in a voice so quiet it was barely a whisper. "The doctors say he might be able to return home happy and healthy within a few months." He didn't respond, waiting for her to finish.

Leila, nervous and red as a beetroot, eventually carried on, gathering together all of her efforts: "I, Mister Knowlton, promise you that I'll pay back cent by cent whatever the sanatorium costs." And, as he kept quiet, struggling to articulate her words, she said: "I promise, Mister Knowlton."

"I'm not interested in getting the money back," he interrupted her abruptly. "You know that already. Don't waste your time playing word games, or humiliating yourself. It won't do you any good."

"Mister Knowlton."

"It's pointless, Leila."

"You can't imagine the hatred I feel for you," she said intensely.

Stephen curved his lips to form a sarcastic smile. "It doesn't bother me, Leila. To be honest, I prefer women to hate me than to come over all sentimental. We're here already." The car stopped in front of the sanatorium. It was a huge white building, surrounded by trees and hidden away at the top of a broad range at the end of a serpentine mountain pass.

Before getting out, she looked at him straight on. Stephen returned her gaze. "Mister Knowlton, have you never wanted to possess the eternal gratitude of an honourable woman?"

"No, Leila. All that stuff makes me laugh."

"I hate you with every bone in my body."

"Well that's a first for me," he said, without boasting. "Up to now, women have always loved me. Women that I'm interested in that is."

"I ..."

"It's all pointless, Leila. The car will be waiting for you tomorrow. You drive it. You'll find a road map on the car seat."

"That's fine," she suddenly exclaimed. "If only you might die before tomorrow." Stephen did nothing other than smile.

* * *

He didn't die. The car was there. It was a dark blue four-seater, amongst the most modern of the models launched by Knowlton factories the previous winter. For a second, before getting into the car, Leila thought about going to see her aunt and telling her everything. But remembering the coldness with which she wished Rob dead ... No, going there and telling her what had happened, that would be another humiliation.... And she'd already faced so much humiliation!

She looked up to the sky, and was blinded by the bright midday sun. "My Lord," she whispered. "Forgive me, don't see a sinner in me. See me for who I am, a victim of fate being tested through pain." She got into the car. As a child, she'd learnt to drive. How wonderful life had been back then! An image of her father suddenly came before her, sitting next to a big window with a smile on his lips. Her mother, slight and pretty, moving happily around a house that was blessed. And then ... everything was over. At that time, she was a happy young girl, but the idyll wasn't built to last. She put the key into the ignition, and had a quick look at the map left on the seat. The car suddenly came to a halt. Leila wasn't familiar with all the dials. Her father had taught her to drive when she was a child, and since then she'd only driven a friend's car when she was seventeen. She tried pressing everything, eventually revving the engine.

It was a beautiful June morning. A morning she'd never forget as long as she lived. At ten in the evening, the dark car stopped in the same place. Leila got out. She closed the door with a single slam, and stared at the car deep in thought. It wasn't cold but Leila nevertheless felt a strange shudder that extended from her head to her toes. She walked down the street determinedly, crossed the road slowly and, instead of heading home, turned into a busy street. When crossing the road, a car-driver, stopped at the traffic lights, looked at her. Leila felt that her entire insides were trembling. Stephen's eyes, those eyes that looked until they scorched, those eyes that burnt her face, blemished her soul. The luxurious car continued on its way. The fiery eyes stopped causing her pain … Leila, as if hypnotized, continued on her way. It was almost eleven by the time she arrived home.

Eve greeted her enthusiastically. "Hello, dear. How's your first day as a nurse gone?"

"It's tired me out." She collapsed into a chair and, much to Eve's surprise, hid her face in her arms and burst into hoarse sobs.

"Leila!"

"Leave me be, Eve. Let me cry."

"But …"

"I need it."

"Leila," Eve whispered, kneeling down in front of her. "Leila, my love. Today was meant to be such a happy day for us." The young woman began to cry again. "Leila."

"I'm … I'm going to bed."

"Without having any dinner?"

"I'm shattered. Absolutely shattered, Eve … If only I could sleep forever. It'd be such a nice feeling, you know?" She stood up, brushed her forehead. "To go to sleep and never wake up."

"Don't say that. Don't say that. Your brother and sisters …"

The two youngest came into the small room, and Leila wiped away the tears with a single swipe. "We've been to see Rob," shouted Martha happily. "Dolly took us. We bought him some story-books and sweets. Rob was very happy."

"Happy, happy …" What a pretty phrase Leila thought. A phrase that could be savoured by the whole world, but not by her. She received them in her arms, and remained still with her mind blank.

* * *

One Thursday, two, ten … At some point, she stopped counting the Thursdays because each and every one ripped away another piece of her life. And, then, when they bumped into each other in the corridors, in the street, in the office patio, as if they were two strangers … Only the fire in his gaze scorched her face. That gaze had turned into an obsession for her. An obsession that stalked her, day and night.

A suitor took a fancy to Leila. She felt belittled, out of place, horrified. Her impeccable morality (Leila would never sin with her spirit) ensured she felt unworthy of masculine admiration. She rejected him. And Dolly, on finding out, asked in shock: "Do you know who you've knocked back?"

"I don't know, and I haven't the slightest interest."

"The best engineer in the Knowlton factories. Will you let me read the letter?"

Leila passed it to her with a gesture of indifference. "He says that he admires me, and would like to take me out."

"Leila … You knocked him back?"

"Yes."

"But, why? Don't you realise?"

"Yes, Dolly. I know just what I'm doing."

Dolly folded the letter up, and left it on the table. "Leila," she said pensively. "You've changed a lot recently. What's up?"

"Nothing."

"Yes, there is Leila. You've been a different person ever since you took Rob to the sanatorium. A trouble shared is a trouble halved. Is Uncle Edward a handful?"

"Bah."

"When they grant me my annual leave, will you let me go with you one Thursday?"

Leila became agitated, blinking in quick succession. With a stifled voice, she said, "Old Edward wouldn't want anyone to accompany me." It was time to clock off. They left together. On crossing the patio, Stephen was getting into his car. Leila didn't look at him. But she felt him like a flame on her back. Dolly took her by the arm, and whispered with surprise: "The way Mister Ogre looks at you."

"Bah."

"If you knew how he was looking at you. Crikey, it's the first time I've really looked into that man's eyes. They're …"

"Would you be quiet?"

The car cruised past them. Stephen didn't look at them.

"Leila, his eyes are like sins and, at the same time, he looked at you with a certain admiration. Does Mister Ogre fancy you?" Dolly, completely unaware of her friend's thoughts, continued by saying: "If he's fallen in love with you, Leila? My girl, him not taking his eyes off you was disconcerting. I don't know much about such things. No guy's ever stopped to look at me, but I'm not stupid. Can you believe I'm trying to imagine Mister Ogre in love? How funny. I can't imagine it. And kissing a woman?"

"Can't you just shut your mouth once and for all?"

"You've become very irritable, my girl. At the end of the day, I can't imagine Mister Ogre would be anything special when it comes to kisses. I'd bet he doesn't know how to."

Leila half-closed her eyes. Doesn't know how to? He knew. And he wasn't an ogre. He was man who perhaps nobody could fathom out, except a woman ... a woman who was his. His and only his. "Dolly, it's cold."

Dolly was confused. "Cold? But, my dear, even the stones are sweating."

"Yes, that's what I meant to say," she said, all disconcerted. "I'm going to catch the bus. I want to see Rob. Tomorrow is Thursday."

"You don't know how sorry I am that I can't come with you, Leila. I've got a hairdresser's appointment. But I'll go tomorrow."

"Thanks Dolly. See you in two days time."

"Yes, until then."

They went their separate ways. Leila took the first bus. She preferred to go alone. But she didn't want to think. Every thought was like a sin. And she was such a sinner! When she crossed a corridor in the sanatorium, one of the nurses said to her: "Your brother has a visitor." A visitor? Who could it be?

She opened the door and froze. It was Stephen. He turned to her and gave a vague smile. In an empty voice, he said: "I've taken the liberty of paying your brother a visit, Miss Leila." She didn't respond. After a pause, she moved towards Rob, leaned towards him and gave him a kiss on the forehead.

"Leila, Mister Knowlton has brought me some really nice books."

"Yes, Rob."

"Leila, I'm very grateful for his visit."

"Yes." She avoided looking at him. So tall, so blonde, so familiar even when he seemed distant, so imposing. That man was like a plague but nevertheless ...

She sensed him leaving. He reappeared at half past nine. "Miss Leila," he said. "You've missed your last bus. I'm going back down now. If you'd like, I can give you a ride."

"Off you go, Leila."

"Yes, my love." She gave Rob another kiss.

Mister Knowlton followed her out. On reaching the door, he turned round and said: "I'll come and see you again, Rob."

"Thanks, Mister Knowlton."

They were now next to each other in the car. He drove. She smoked a cigarette. Leila was more beautiful than ever that night, a shade of melancholy darkening her pretty clear eyes with a silvery grey touch. "There's no need for you to visit my brother," she said out of the blue.

"Maybe I did so out of curiosity."

"Rob doesn't want your curiosity."

"I visited him because I wanted to."

"Tell me something I don't know. You always do just as you please." He looked at her. "The world is yours. Has it ever occurred to you that one day you might be denied something you want more than anything?"

"If and when that happens, I'll fight for it." They didn't exchange another word. When the car came to a stop in front of Leila's house, she got out and said: "Good night."

CHAPTER IX

~

The impassioned suitor who'd stalked Leila ever since he'd sent her that first note was called John Steiner, and was one of the most valued engineers in the Knowlton empire. On one particular evening, as Leila left work accompanied by Dolly, John respectfully and gallantly approached her just as she was leaving the building.

"Miss Leila, I'm still waiting for an answer to the notes I've sent you. Have I offended you in some way?"

Dolly made herself scarce, disappearing amongst a group of fellow employees. Leila had no choice but to face the engineer. "I've received them, Mister Steiner."

"Call me John."

"And you haven't offended me, John."

"Thanks, Miss Leila. Do I have your permission to call you by your Christian name?"

"You do."

"Will you also permit me to accompany you home?" He raised his shoulders. At that precise moment, Stephen's car went past them. Leila didn't look, but she knew that Stephen's eyes would be drilling into her. "Leila," John said fervently, "I love you. I've loved you ever since I first set eyes on you. Before approaching you, I thought about it long and hard."

"John."

"Don't say anything to me now. Think about it. I am not a man to take rash decisions. Nor do I demand them of others. I like to think things through, and I like to let others do the same."

"In any case …"

"Give it some thought, Leila. I beg you. I'm not suggesting a casual fling," he added respectfully. "I'm talking about marriage." Marriage, as if she could wed! It was as if her heart was shrinking and, at the same time, she felt a mortal hatred towards those tragic Thursdays in her life. Leila would have liked to marry and have children, to be happy with a good and decent man, like John for example. A man who would love her intensely, who would inject a little bit of happiness into her life. But fate didn't hold that little bit of happiness in store for her. Fate was, for her, something of a nightmare.

"Leila, did you hear what I said?" Yes, she had heard him and, for a moment she wanted to believe she was a young woman like any other, with no worries, happy and confident she'd find the love of her life. "Leila."

"Yes, John, I heard you perfectly," and, with the delicacy that was her greatest charm, "I don't think you know that I have three young siblings …"

"I know everything."

She looked at him quickly. For a moment, she thought that "everything" referred to her great sin. "Everything?" she asked, almost mumbling.

"What you do for your siblings. How you struggle to offer Rob the possibility of a future …"

"Ah!"

"And I want to share that struggle with you."

"You're a very good man, John."

"I'm a man in love."

"But I can't accept your sacrifice."

"You're wrong. To me it's not a sacrifice. Quite the opposite in fact. It would be my pleasure to help you live. Let me accompany you on this life-long journey. But don't give me an answer now. Think it over."

"John, I …"

"No, no," he interrupted her softly. "Take your time."

"I'd like to tell you."

"I'd rather you thought it over." And before she had the chance to react, he grabbed hold of her hand, kissed her fervently, and said: "Give me an answer when you've had the chance to mull things over. Good evening, Leila."

She watched him walk off into the distance. Leila sighed. She didn't love him, nor could she ever love him, but it was reassuring to know that a good decent man really loved her, and had asked her to follow him on the thorny road that is life. Leila did an about turn and headed home. She walked as if she were blind, hypnotized, and she didn't even notice a man climbing out of his car and blocking her way. He didn't say anything as he stopped in front of Leila, giving that look that burnt right into her. She was stopped still in her tracks.

"Let that be the last time," he said with a noticeably agitated voice.

She felt rebellious. At that moment, she would have given years of her life in exchange for money, so as to be able to throw note by note what he'd paid for Rob in his face. She limited herself to saying: "Get out of my way."

"Don't ever forget, Leila. The last time."

Leila didn't respond. She walked round him and scurried up the stairs like a woman possessed.

* * *

She was at work. It was a Saturday. Dolly was eating a sandwich, and flicking through the newspaper. "For once, it's their turn."

Leila looked up from her typewriter and asked: "What was that?"

Dolly was eating as if there were no tomorrow, fearful that someone would discover her with the huge ham sandwich. "I'm talking about what's in the society pages of today's newspaper. And I was saying that rich folk have to go some time."

"Who's died?"

"That old maid with millions, the one who has your surname is on her way out."

Leila jumped, only to then remain still as a statue, her face pale and expressionless, as if she had been tied to her seat. "She's ... dying?" she asked with her mouth wide open.

Dolly folded the newspaper up, cleaned her hands and exclaimed joyfully: "I can't go without a sandwich at this time of the day. I've got a well-disciplined stomach."

"Who's dying?"

"That super-rich woman. She's about to die following a long cancerous ailment. About time they suffered, isn't it?"

"Don't be ... cruel." Leila wanted to cry. Not exactly for her aunt. But she had been her only living relative, her father's sister. And, in any case, she was a human being.

"It's quite something. And would you believe it? The newspaper says that, on her deathbed, all she does is call after her dog. These rich folks are stupid. It also says that she has a colossal fortune and no relatives to inherit. It looks as if everything will go to the dog. Why doesn't someone send that dog to my house? It'd be great if I were chosen to look after that wealthy canine."

"Don't be so quick to mock, Dolly. It's ... cruel."

Dolly looked at her and started to laugh. "Anyone would say the news affected you, my dear. It just makes me laugh. With so many human beings without a dollar to their name, starving and freezing, and that crazy old bat leaves everything to a dog. If she weren't almost dead, I'd say she should hang for it."

At that moment, the voice of one of the secretaries came over the intercom: "Miss Leila, Mister Knowlton is waiting for you in his office." She shuddered. He never called her. What could he want from her at that moment? The mere thought of seeing him made her shiver all over. That man was a nightmare, a fear, a pernicious pleasure that one somehow still desires. Her grand obsession!

"Don't just stand there, Leila." Dolly woke her from her daze: "Didn't you hear? Mister Ogre has summoned you."

"I'm on my way."

"Someone else who's not right in the head," moaned Dolly. "What does that bachelor get up to? Who is he thinking of leaving his millions to when he dies? Because that one will die alone. I don't see him being capable of saying a tender phrase to a lady."

Leila stood up. She didn't respond. She thought. A tender phrase? He didn't pronounce them. He was a passionate man, domineering, silent, but ... he knew how to love. Yes; in his heart there was an unlimited supply of tenderness, you could tell from his silences. Something that perhaps nobody knew, nobody apart from her...

She left her desk without uttering a sound, and went down the corridor towards the elevator. When she knocked on the door, her legs were trembling. A female secretary opened the door. He looked indifferent, sat behind the giant desk with his glasses concealing the blinding shine of his ashen-grey eyes.

"Come in, Miss Leila," he said in an impersonal tone of voice. She moved towards him and waited in front of his desk. "Please, do take a seat."

She didn't sit down. "What do you want from me, Mister Knowlton?" she asked in an impersonal manner. And she felt as if her face were on fire. The flames that came from within and spread out like burning larva across her face.

He made a gesture and his secretaries left the room in silence. When the door had closed behind the last one, he exclaimed as if he were about to explode: "Take a seat."

"I'm not sitting down."

"Leila, you are testing my patience." She didn't respond. "Do you know why I've called you here?" And his tone changed: "So that you can spend tomorrow, Sunday, with Uncle Edward."

She shuddered as if assailed by a thousand demons. Her rebellious spirit revolted. "No," she said energetically. "No."

"It's an order."

"And I've said no. You already know."

He turned around, stood up and came out from behind the desk. He stood right in front of Leila, his figure towering over her. "Leila, I don't know what's happening to me."

"After the way you've treated me and the state you've left me in, you can't expect me to help work out whatever you're going through."

"You're to blame for everything I'm going through. Your coldness, your rebelliousness ... they are like hooks that reel me in on a daily basis. Would you," he whispered, "would you like to marry me?"

The answer left no room for confusion; as if it were a bullet, Leila shot out: "No."

"Leila!"

"No!"

"You're crazy, you silly girl."

"I might be crazy. If I am, you're to blame. I'd choose the most wretched beggar over you. And do you know why?" she hardened for a few moments. "You don't know why? Well I'll tell you. Because I know you're happy by my side. Because you love me. That's why I won't marry you. Because you're the last man in the world I'd make happy. You have of me that which you've taken, but to give you something of my own free will ... No, oh no! You still don't know me." And, without waiting for a reply, she did an about turn and headed for the door. Stephen blocked her passage. He took her by the hand and, without saying a word, held her against his chest. He moved towards her and kissed her in that way.

"Yes," he whispered. "You've become what I need most in this world. And, Leila, what I take from you no longer satisfies that need. Take pleasure in my submission if you want. The big boss asking mercy of a humble employee. Laugh," he said bitterly. "It's the truth. I want your heart. And the mere idea of thinking about you with another man drives me crazy. Out of charity," he added, defeated, "forget all the harm I've done to you, and imagine you were my wife ever since that very first visit to Uncle Edward."

"Let me go."

"Whatever you love the most in this world, I'll offer you in exchange."

"My brother and sisters are all that I love. You've seen that clearly enough, haven't you? You've seen for yourself the sacrifices I've been willing to make. Well, not even for them will I forgive you," and, with regret: "I would have admired and loved you Stephen. It's ... not hard to fall in love with a man like you. A man," she smiled sarcastically, "who everyone considers incapable of love and of whose love I am perhaps the only woman to know anything. But you've been merciless, Stephen. You took me in exchange for some banknotes, and I ... will repay you every last cent. I don't know when. Someday. And then, Stephen ... I won't want to ever see you again. Now let me go." She forced herself free of his grasp energetically, and remained stiff in front of him, as if made of stone. "Now you know what I think."

"Yes," he admitted. "Perhaps I did you much harm. But I don't know what you feel."

"What I feel doesn't count," she said blinking. "If I spoke to you of it, it would rip me in two, you know that." She put her hand on the door-handle.

"I've spoken to my mother about you. She wants to meet you."

"Let me through, Stephen. I have no desire to meet your mother. And when Rob comes out of the sanatorium ... I'll leave this firm. I'll go far away ... And, as far as I'll be concerned, you'll be something akin to a nightmare for which I'll be held to account on the day of judgment."

"Leila."

"Now you know. If you still want me to visit your uncle ..."

"Yes, always."

"You've no mercy."

"I love you. It's not something ... I can do anything about."

"Wait."

At that moment the intercom came on. "Leila," said Dolly in an agitated voice. "I don't know what's happening at your home, but they've asked you to return without delay." Leila ran out without giving Stephen a second glance. By the time he tried to stop her, she was already inside the elevator, breathless. Without returning to her desk, the young woman went out onto the street and caught the first taxi she chanced upon.

When she opened the door to her home, she could hardly breathe. "Eve … Eve," she shouted. Aunt Marie's maid came to meet her, followed by Eve. "Ah!" Leila exclaimed, understanding the situation. "It's you, Rita."

"Yes, Miss Leila. My mistress has summoned you urgently." She added with sadness: "She's dying. Did you know?"

"Yes, I knew. Let's see," and looking at Eve. "Take care of the children, Eve. If I'm not able to come later, I'll let you know. Rita, let's go." And, inside Aunt Marie's luxurious saloon, Leila said bitterly: "I thought Aunt Marie only called out to her dog."

"Suddenly, she stopped uttering his name. And she screamed for you to come."

CHAPTER X

～

"Aunt Marie!," kneeling down at her bedside, taking the invalid's hand in hers.

Half-opening her eyes and barely mustering a whisper, she responded "Leila, my darling, tell me that you forgive me."

"With all my heart, Aunt Marie."

"I've been cruel to your siblings. And to your father and his wife. I've lived alone, Leila. Completely isolated. Nature didn't give me much. All I've had is money, wealth galore ... But money can't buy you love ... I," she added, overwhelmed with emotion, "could have had four children, you and your siblings. If I could live my life again, Leila ... But that's not possible."

"Quiet now, Aunt Marie. Get some rest."

"Right away, darling. As soon as our conversation has finished, I'll rest for all eternity." They were alone in the giant room. In the antechamber, which Leila had rushed through without greeting anyone, there were many people: lawyers, partners, friends, extremely elegant women. None of them knew of the existence of that niece, the daughter of the invalid's brother. When she crossed the antechamber, some of them glanced at each other, but nobody asked any questions. Only one gentleman (the notary) raised a tepid smile, but he didn't say anything. The doctor was getting impatient. Nobody had called him into Miss Heimer's chamber, and he knew she had only minutes to live.

Aunt Marie was also aware of the fact and, speaking so quietly that Leila had to move closer in order to make out her words, said: "Leila, my darling Leila."

"What is it, Aunt Marie?"

"A few days ago, I changed my will in your favour. I've left everything I own to you. Stop working straight away, ask that they move your siblings here, and don't leave my side until they bury me. And mourn a little for me, Leila. Let one genuine tear rest on my corpse."

Leila had already begun to cry. And not because her aunt had asked her to, but because it came naturally. Because she had a heart, she was affected by her aunt's state and extended the hand of compassion just when Marie needed it most. "Hush now, and rest, Aunty. I beg you, please."

"You will never have money troubles ever again, Leila. You'll have everything," and with a sarcasm that hadn't deserted her even in her final hour: "and that'll show you how vile the world really is. You'll realize that money is a marvellous key that opens every door. The city of Springfield will kneel down before you. And those who ignored you and made you suffer will be humbled, they'll seek out your company and flatter you. Don't pay any attention to such flattery, Leila. Live for yourself and your siblings. I've been vain and a queer fish. And, as you can see, I'm dying alone," and she added with regret: "There are men and women behind that door. Do they appreciate me? Ignore them. They are vain creatures like me, who feel proud at the time of my death to be able to say: 'We are friends of the deceased, an extremely wealthy lady.' But nobody will say: 'We are her true friends, she has our respect and affection as a person.' I've also been like that, Leila. Don't ever go down that route, Leila."

"Quiet now, Aunty. You'll run out of breath."

"What does it matter," she whispered as if pausing to take breath. "Nothing matters now, my dear, apart from you being at my side and crying for my passing. Don't ... wear black, or drape morbid ribbons on the balconies of my mansion. Don't adorn my grave with ostentatious displays of grief. A bunch of flowers that have been cut by you ... in the garden, and your heartfelt tears, Leila. Because ... I know ... they are genuine."

* * *

"Who is that pretty young girl with the bunch of flowers?" asked Gisela Knowlton, leaning towards another glamorous woman sitting beside her.

"Marie's niece."

"Ah! She had relatives?"

"So it seems."

"I never knew."

"She, I'm sure, would have been all too aware of the fact."

Leila deposited the bunch of flowers on Aunt Marie's body, making the sign of the cross. Two tears slithered down from her eyes. She left the room and headed upstairs. She pushed a door. Rita and Eve were trying to calm the two children down. The kids, on seeing Leila, ran frightened to her side. "What's going on, Leila? I'm scared," cried the youngest. "I want us to go home."

Leila put her hand through the child's hair, and caressed it. "Glad, from today onwards, we are going to live here."

"Here," she spat out. "In this huge house."

"Yes, my darling. And Rob will come as well. We'll set him up in the room on the ground floor that catches the sun. And the best specialists will visit him here."

"Ah, superb!"

"Now obey Rita and Eve, and remain in silence."

"Are you leaving?"

"I must, Glad. Aunt Marie has died, and I need to be at her side."

It was all like a nightmare. An exhausting day she would never forget. An endless succession of people who looked her up and down as if she were an object. People who held out their hands to offer their condolences. Glamorous ladies spoke of the deceased, listing her virtues. Nobody recalled her defects. It was better that way. Neither did Leila recall them apart from on watching her brother and sisters dine in that huge dining hall at midday, when she began to dwell on the pointlessness of her sacrifice. She might have a lot of money but she, in spite of everything, was a dead woman as far as love was concerned. A being who would go through life burdened with the horrific nightmare of mortal sin. And if she were to marry Stephen, to then live far away from him? Why not? She'd have to talk it over with the house chaplain. When everything was finished, when she was alone with her conscience, she'd go to Father Andrés's quarters, and she'd tell him … Yes, she'd tell him everything and unload all the pain of the failure that was her life.

* * *

"Stephen, you already know the news. Don't you?"

"What news?" he asked distractedly.

"The death of Miss Marie. I've just come from there."

"I read about it in the newspapers." And he carried on eating, served by a tense waiter. A young maid stood still behind the lady, who added: "You'll have to go and offer your condolences. I was a close friend of the deceased."

"Condolences? To whom? The dog?"

"Now that you say that, I missed out the most important bit. Miss Marie has a blood relative, a niece."

"Ah!"

"Aren't you surprised?" Stephen, as inexpressive as ever, just shrugged his shoulders. He was in no position to be thinking about other people's lives when his heart and brain were exclusively preoccupied by the most important concern in his life. "She's a really pretty young thing. Thin, nice-looking, well-dressed. Very distinguished. I swear, Stephen, we were all so surprised, as nobody knew anything about such a niece. She's moved into the mansion and, when her eyes filled up with tears, they seemed genuine. I took to the girl. She has a melancholy expression, as if something were constantly weighing her down."

"You're very observant," he said for want of anything better to say.

"Aren't you going to go and offer your condolences?"

"Yes, I'll pass by on my way to the office."

On arriving at work, a secretary passed him an envelope. "What's this?"

"It was delivered just now, Sir."

He played around with the envelope in his hands. It was hefty, and felt as if it might contain money. He opened it hurriedly, and was left white as a ghost. "Leave, now," he ordered with an agitated voice. When the door closed behind the secretary, he took Leila's note in his trembling hands and read: "Herewith is all the money you spent on Rob. My debt to you is settled. Leila." He swivelled in his chair and switched on the intercom. With an agitated voice, he spoke as he had never done before: "Miss Leila, come up, right away."

Mister Leigh answered: "Miss Leila and Miss Dolly have just offered their resignations."

"What?"

"That's all we know, Sir!"

"But …" Mister Leigh listened to his boss in an altered state. An unusually altered state for a man who was frosty temperance incarnate. "Do you know why?"

"No, Mister Knowlton. I'm surprised." The intercom was switched off. Stephen stood up. He crumpled the bank notes between his fingers and strode out of the office.

The secretaries commented amongst themselves: "He looks like he's gone mad. We've never seen him like this before."

The man who was the subject of office gossip drove his car through the streets, as if the devil himself were in pursuit. He stopped the car in front of Leila's house. Taking two steps at a time, he walked up to her front door on which he knocked with desperation. Nobody answered. A neighbour came out and said: "Don't bother knocking. They've all left."

"Where to?"

"I don't know Sir. An elegant saloon came to pick them all up."

John Steiner! Oh, no! There wasn't a man on earth capable of taking Leila away from him. He got back in his car and returned to the factory. Moments later, John Steiner the engineer was urgently summoned to the boss's office. Surprised, he went straight away.

"John … where is Miss Leila?"

The engineer shrugged his shoulders. "I have no idea, Sir."

"She's not at home," said Stephen, losing his aristocratic composure. "And she's resigned from her job."

"I haven't seen her for days, Mister Knowlton."

"You … were chasing after her."

"Yes, that's right. But she rejected me, not leaving me with the slightest glimmer of hope."

"You can leave now."

"Anything else, Sir?"

"Nothing," he grumbled. "Return to your work."

On being left alone, Stephen stood up and paced up and down his office with restless agitation. What had happened to him, the man who had always laughed about the love of women. And, like a schoolboy, he'd fallen for the charms of that girl who, next to him, was nothing, but refused to yield. Yes, perhaps that was it. Because she was different. Because she continued to be essentially pure, in spite of everything. With that kind of purity incapable of being blemished by anyone. And it belonged to her. Nobody could take it from her, and Leila needed to understand that her duty was to marry him. The phone rang. "Yes."

"Is that you, Stephen?" asked a voice that belonged to his mother.

"Yes."

"Have you been to offer your condolences?"

"It slipped my mind."

"You must go, Stephen. It's your duty, and it's the polite thing to do."

"I'll go … I'll go … for God's sake."

"What's up with you, son? You've been unbearable for a while now."

"No, nothing's up with me."

"Alright, alright … Go to the Heimers' place. The funeral is almost upon us, and as I can't go …"

"I'll go as soon as I can," Stephen barked. And he hung up. Half an hour later, feeling as if his head was about to explode, he parked his car behind a row of vehicles that stretched across the entire square in front of the mighty residence of the deceased Miss Heimer. Stephen crossed the park without looking anywhere specific. The house was crammed full of people. He hated convention but, as an important member of Springfield society, it was incumbent upon him to carry out that courtesy. He crossed a room, and the first thing he saw was the chaplain don Andrés and … Dolly.

"Good afternoon," he said as a greeting. Stephen kissed don Andrés's hand, before fixing his piercing stare on Dolly. "What are you doing here?" he asked with venom.

"I no longer work in your offices, Mister Knowlton," Dolly replied calmly. "I resigned earlier this afternoon."

"And may I ask why?"

"I found a better way to spend my days."

"And … your friend?"

"The same. I'm sorry, I'm in a hurry." And, after smiling at the priest, Dolly made her exit.

"I want to offer my condolences to the niece of the deceased, don Andrés."

"Yes, yes, Stephen. That's what I imagined. Follow that corridor. You'll find Miss Heimer alone in the room at the end."

"Thank you." And he headed in that direction.

CHAPTER XI

She was, as he had been told, alone, with her head against the glass of the giant window. The door had been left ajar, and Stephen only had to push it for his eyes to feast on Leila's back. "Leila," he called.

She turned around as if she had been prodded by a thousand demons. "You?"

"And, you. What are you doing here?"

"I'm Miss Heimer's niece."

Stephen moved forward as if propelled by a hurricane only to then stand rigidly in front of her. "... You ... the niece of ...?" "That's why you've sent me ...?"

"Yes, that's why."

"Leila ..."

"I accept your condolences," she said coldly, "because I suppose that's the reason for you coming here."

"Yes, but."

"Thank you, Mister Knowlton."

"Leila, would you please stop this play-acting."

"I'm not play-acting. I'm the niece of an extremely wealthy lady, who died yesterday last thing at night. It's a pity, Stephen, that my aunt was so proud or that she didn't die sooner. At least that way, your soul and mine would have been saved."

"Listen. Conventions and polite conversation don't mean anything to me. Nor am I bothered about your money or what must have gone on between you and your aunt such that she never mentioned you. The only thing I know is that I can't live without you, and if you don't marry me, I'll make public your visits, and the real reason for you going to the mountain lodge."

She shuddered. "You wouldn't, Stephen. If you do ..."

"I will! And bear in mind that you're no longer some anonymous girl. It won't be long until the newspapers start reporting on how often you close the bathroom door."

"Stephen, I once called you a monster ..."

"Yes, some time ago. There have been many days of sun and rain since then. When I kissed you ... I remember, Leila," he whispered gently: "I never wanted you to be just another fling. From day one I knew I wouldn't be able to live without you. And you love me too. You're too much of a child. You didn't know what love was until you made me an offering of your blessed purity."

"Shut up, Stephen."

"I'll shut up, and I'll go now … But don't forget what I've said to you."

"I'll hate you."

"I'd rather your hatred than to lose you completely." And he walked out. Leila collapsed into a sofa and remained there as if she'd been knocked out cold. The sound of voices gradually tailed off, and it started to get dark. It was the height of summer, but Leila felt cold.

"Leila," said the voice of don Andrés.

She was startled. "Come in, Father."

"Alone and in darkness. And you've let your aunt be taken away without bidding her a final farewell," he reproached her. "Your friend and I had to be in multiple places at the same time in order to attend to the many friends who came to pay their respects."

"Come, Father. Sit down next to me, and don't scold me."

"Have you something to say to me, young lady? I have sensed it since you knelt down in front of the altar this morning without taking communion." Leila burst into tears. She needed to cry. She cried a lot, with desperation. "Calm down, calm down," instructed don Andrés, sitting opposite her and looking in the shadow cast by her bent-over figure. "Unburden your soul, my dear child."

"The thing is …" She suddenly started to talk. From when her father had died to that moment, she'd always spoken with succinct phrases, saying no more than was strictly necessary. On finishing, without omitting the smallest detail, there was silence. It was she who interrupted it to say: "That's why, because I remembered everything this afternoon, as if living through it once again, I wasn't next to my aunt when they took her away."

"I understand."

"My duty."

"Sometimes duty doesn't matter, Leila. You're a simple and decent soul. Sin doesn't corrode your spirit." And, decisively, "Tomorrow, I'll give you communion, and you can marry the day afterwards."

"Me, get married?"

"It's your duty."

"But, Father …"

"You have confessed to me, Leila. My absolution will come with the promise of your forthcoming wedding." Leila lowered her head, not answering. The priest stood up, made the sign of the cross above the feminine head and softly said: "Let's eat, my girl, and forget everything that's happened. I can't reproach you for anything, because you were bound by affection towards your poor brother. But don't forget that it was your duty to have come before committing the sin. Nevertheless, God Our Lord will forgive you, because He, better than you or I, knows that the sin has not tarnished your spirit.

* * *

Stephen was there, kneeling down next to her. Father Andrés officiated the mass. Dolly was also there (without understanding anything), as were Leila's sisters, alongside a nearly recovered Rob, radiant to be reunited with his siblings. They took communion and then had breakfast together in the huge dining room. Dolly talked and talked without pausing for breath, as was her wont. She continued to live with Leila in the capacity of housekeeper. The children talked about their things. The priest gave advice. And, when Leila left the dining room, Stephen followed her, making his excuses.

"What's going on here, Father?" Dolly asked, cutting to the quick as was her way.

"These things happen, Dolly. They're going to get married ..."

"To get what ...?"

"Married."

"It's impossible."

"It's not."

"And why? I just don't understand."

"There are many things which will never be understood ..." smiled the priest beatifically. "But they happen."

"That is true. Are they ... in love?"

"Yes," he said without the slightest hint of doubt. And he wasn't lying. He could read it in their hearts. Stephen, with whom he had spoken the night before, didn't deny the love that was evident. Quite the opposite, he proclaimed it effusively. She, Leila, didn't speak of it, but you could sense it and the elderly priest thought words were hardly ever necessary.

"It's incredible, Father."

"Yes, it is. Do I have your permission to return to my quarters, my child?"

"Yes, of course, Father. I'll look after the children. Come on Rob, time for you to be in bed. And, you two, go and play at Rob's side."

* * *

"Leila ..."

"Don't say anything. Father Andrés will tell you I have no objection to marrying you. But then ..."

"Hush, Leila. Don't offend our past any longer. You ... love me." He turned around quickly, his eyes glistening. His cheeks were bright red.

"And even if that were the case, what difference would it make?"

"It's ... a blessing."

"I'll never be yours, Stephen. Never! I'm marrying out of duty ... My love will be a combination of hatred and scorn. Something akin to a well-deserved divine punishment."

"Let's not argue. We'll go and see my mother this evening. I've spoken to her about you."

"I don't want to have anything to do with you or your life. I've seen you at your cruellest, and I'd rather continue seeing you that way."

"There are too many things in common, my little Leila. Don't you see?"

"Leave me be, Stephen. I beg you."

"I'll come and find you this evening."

"I'll be rude to your mother."

"So be it. I'm still taking you home." He went towards her. Leila moved away. She fluttered her eyelids as if not wanting to set eyes on him. But she saw him. He was imprinted in her very being, as if he were a wound. A wound that caused insufferable pain. "Leila," he whispered next to her. "Leila, forget the damage I've done to you. Think of how we could start again, getting off on a completely different footing."

"Shut up."

"Start again, darling. I'll dedicate the rest of my life to making up for what I've done."

"Leave me alone. I beg you in the name of whatever you love the most."

"I love you above all else."

"Well, in my name then."

"Let me kiss you."

"No!" And she fled like a crazy woman to the other end of the room. His kisses … Those kisses that were her greatest pleasure. Yes, yes, although she didn't want to admit it, that was the truth. She would never be able to forget Stephen's kisses, those first kisses that humiliated her but, at the same time, were a blessing for her.

"Leila …"

"Go away."

"Yes, I'm going. But I'll be back. And you'd have to be made of stone, which you're not, to reward my devotion with hatred." He moved away. She cried, defeated, collapsed in the sofa. Money? Yes, more than she could ever want. She could dedicate every waking hour for the rest of her life to throwing notes over the balcony, and it wouldn't run out. And for what? What good was the money doing her?

* * *

Stephen's luxurious residence was quite a distance away. His mother was radiant with happiness. Leila needed to be polite and even affectionate, and she felt the warm kisses of Gisela Knowlton on her face. Those were the kind of familial kisses that mark sincerity.

The car continued on its journey. Stephen drove. She was at his side, silent and pretty, completely exhausted.

"Will we go … there?"

"No!"

"Tomorrow, when we are man and wife."

"No."

"Leila, be reasonable."

"No!"

Without bringing the car to a halt, he put an arm over his shoulders and moved it towards her. "Little Leila, pretty Leila. You need to understand me …"

"If I beg you that you leave me in my home …"

"Well promise me."

"Nothing."

"Tell me that tomorrow …"

"No!"

"Never?"

"I don't know. I'm … I'm … it's as if I were born again today. Or if I'd died and been resuscitated at this very moment."

"I'm resuscitated by your side." And his lips smiled albeit slightly for the first time since that very first Thursday.

*   *   *

The car drove off into the horizon. Father Andrés smiled gently and contemplated with deep consternation the black car as it moved into the distance until disappearing towards the twilight grey of the evening sky.

"They were made for each other," Gisela said from behind.

The priest turned round and, hiding his hands beneath the pockets of his well-worn cassock, said slowly: "Let's hope that turns out to be true." He didn't express them, but he had his doubts. Leila was a pure soul, yes. But she was rebellious, spiritual, and Stephen Knowlton had reached her by a misguided route. Leila loved him. Don Andrés knew that, but … he also knew she had been vilely obliged to commit an act she would regret for the rest of her life, and that nightmare would sour her love in a million different ways.

*   *   *

"Let's go," said Stephen, looking tenderly at the woman who was now his wife, "to Uncle Edward's house." She didn't respond. "Leila, did you hear me?"

"Yes."

"Shall we go?" The car was driving down the highway. Leila could see the mountain. Her stationary eyes suddenly blinked. "Leila … shall we go or not?"

"Yes," she finally said in a somewhat stifled tone of voice. "Let's go." And off they went. I invite you, dear readers, to follow me with *Leila's Indecision*, the second part of this novel.[1]

---

[1] The rights for the English language translation of *Los jueves de Leila* were generously donated by the estate of Corín Tellado.

MHRA New Translations

The guiding principle of this series is to publish new translations into English of important works that have been hitherto imperfectly translated or that are entirely untranslated. The work to be translated or re-translated should be aesthetically or intellectually important. The proposal should cover such issues as copyright and, where relevant, an account of the faults of the previous translation/s; it should be accompanied by independent statements from two experts in the field attesting to the significance of the original work (in cases where this is not obvious) and to the desirability of a new or renewed translation.

Translations should be accompanied by a fairly substantial introduction and other, briefer, apparatus: a note on the translation; a select bibliography; a chronology of the author's life and works; and notes to the text.

Titles will be selected by members of the Editorial Board and edited by leading academics.

Andrew Counter
General Editor

Editorial Board

Professor Malcolm Cook (French)
Professor Alison Finch (French)
Andrew Counter (French)
Professor Ritchie Robertson (Germanic)
Dr Mark Davie (Italian)
Dr Stephen Parkinson (Portuguese)
Professor David Gillespie (Slavonic)
Dr Duncan Wheeler (Spanish)
Professor Jonathan Thacker (Spanish)

For details of how to order please visit our website at:
www.translations.mhra.org.uk

Lightning Source UK Ltd.
Milton Keynes UK
UKOW06f1706240917
309775UK00026B/249/P